FILTHY VOWS

ALESSANDRA TORRE

filthy
VOWS

Editing: Marion Making Manuscripts

Proofreading: JO's Book Addiction

Cover Design: Perfect Pear Creative Covers

This one is for the Brads and the Elles.

PROLOGUE

"Are you sure about this?" My husband stood before me and put his finger under my chin, lifting it until my eyes met his. I wet my lips, the taste of champagne still on them, and nodded.

"Open your knees."

Gripping the edge of the bed, I parted my legs, the silky fabric of my dress clinging to my inner thighs. His gaze dropped to the motion, and I could see his want battling with a reluctancy to take this next step.

He sank to his knees before me. Running his hand down to my calf, he gave the muscle a possessive squeeze before undoing the satin strap of my right stiletto. Carefully, he removed the expensive shoe and set it aside, then moved to the left. In the dim bedroom light, I watched his features tighten in attentive concentration as his strong hands made quick work of the delicate heels.

My bare feet settled on the wood floor as he ran his palms reverently up my bare legs, stopping at my open knees. His gaze flicked to mine. "Wider," he said hoarsely, and pushed my knees further apart.

I yielded, allowing him to stretch my legs open and lift my

dress, draping it outside of my knees so that I was fully exposed. He smiled when he saw my lack of panties, and ran a tender hand across my damp folds. His fingers spread me, then pushed so deeply inside that the platinum glint of his wedding ring disappeared. I gasped at the intrusion and his eyes darkened at how wet and needy I was. "Tell me what you want."

I met his eyes. "Him."

He swore and his fingers withdrew, then pushed back in, pumping across my neediest point. "Where?"

"Right here. On our bed."

My eyes dropped and I could see the instant and impressive response of his cock, stiffening at my words.

"When?"

I looked past him and at the man who sat against our dresser, his shoulders hunched, hands gripping the edge of the mahogany. His eyes met mine and he stood, his face tight with hunger and want.

"Now."

1

---

7 years earlier

ELLE

I used to be nonchalant about penises. Truth be told, I thought they were ugly. Misshapen. I had the same offhand relationship with them that I did with my period. A sort of *oh. You again. I guess I can deal with you, assuming you aren't too much of a pain*. I'd dealt with seven penises before I heard about Easton North's cock. The four-letter word had been so out of place at the long sorority house table that I'd choked on a crisp chunk of broccoli and had to chug a half-glass of iced tea just to wash it free.

"Chelsea," I chided, glancing around the dining hall for our sharp-nosed house mother. She had an uncanny ability to sniff out foul language, smuggled alcohol, and the smell of weed—all violations that carried strict punishments and monetary fines. Chelsea was already on her shit list, a situation the short blonde had dismissed with one toss of her French-manicured hand.

"It's true, Elle." she insisted, oblivious to the way her sing-song voice carried. "I'm telling you, it was the prettiest thing I've ever seen."

"Pretty?" Laura examined the piece of salmon draped over her salad with the intensity of a surgeon. "That's an interesting word to use."

I agreed, though to agree with Laura Pinn was paramount to social suicide. Agreement meant servitude, and once she sniffed out a potential flunky, she hunted and corralled them with the ruthlessness of a hyena.

"It was just..." Chelsea sank against the back of the linen-wrapped chair and sighed, her features settling into the blissful look of a woman who has just gorged on too many desserts. I watched her with interest. "Perfection." She finished. "Thick, beautiful, perfection."

I swallowed my own questions, certain that they would be covered by others. Sure enough, Ling perked up, lifting her attention off the thick calculus book before her and fixating on Chelsea. "I thought you were dating that soccer player."

"I was," Chelsea mused. "But that was before Easton. Before I met IT."

IT seemed to be a reference to his cock. I shook a packet of Splenda into my tea and waited, curious to see where this conversation was going.

She groaned. "You guys know me. It's not like I have a thing for cocks. It's just something about *his*." She lifted her gaze to the ceiling and smiled as if picturing it above her.

There was a long period of stunned silence where we digested the fact that Chelsea didn't think she had a thing for dicks. The girl was our pledge class whore. She was the reason we scored the section 13 football block with Delt, the reason our house curfew had been changed to midnight, and the sole cause of a sorority-wide three-hour standards lecture on promiscuity. At one point poor Ling, who'd never been to second base, had blushed so deep that the speaker had stopped in alarm, certain she was choking.

"You don't have a thing for cocks?" I repeat, lowering my voice on the final word. "So..." I didn't want to say it. I didn't want to blurt out the question hammering inside every one of our sophomoric heads. *So... why do you sleep with every guy who crosses your path?*

Chelsea straightened off the back of the chair and the overhead light glinted off a whitehead heavily coated in concealer. "I suppose you've been having sex with Jonah because you like his penis?" She said dryly.

It was a valid point and I snapped my lips together, dropping my gaze off her whitehead and back to my salad. I was having sex with Jonah because I liked Jonah, and sex seemed to be that eventual outcome of any college relationship that survived three weeks. Jonah's penis, out of the seven I'd seen, was the smallest—an observation I'd made to Chelsea in the back of a filthy cab, at 2:30 in the morning, drunk on tequila. An observation I'd hoped she had forgotten. She hadn't.

"*Why* is his penis so pretty?" Ling tilted her head, peering at Chelsea as she speared a cucumber from her bowl without looking. "Color? Texture? Girth? Shape?"

Only Ling would ask about the texture of a penis, and Laura Pinn swooped on the opportunity, talons outstretched.

"Ling," she sniffed. "Why don't you take your studying into the den and let the big girls talk?" She gave a delicate and generous smile, the sort that the wolf flashed right before he ate Little Red Riding Hood.

I clamped a hand on Ling's arm before she could move. "Fuck off, Laura." I gave my own sweet smile. "Chelsea?" I raised my brows, urging her to answer the question before Laura Pinn blew a blood vessel.

Chelsea's gaze darted between the three of us like a freshman jaw on its first hit of cocaine. I could tell she was torn between the potential carnage of an impending fight and the juiciness of her story. She let me hang for one painful second, then sighed, that starstruck look returning to her eyes. "Okay, so you know how some heads are, like, mushrooms on the top of a shaft?"

At Ling's horrified look, she carried on, redirecting the next question to me.

"And how others are smaller than the shaft, like a pencil eraser?"

I nodded, though I had never examined my penises to this extent. Most of my interactions with them had been in the dark, my hand sweaty, contact minimal, the experiences short. Out of my seven, I could have potentially picked out three in a lineup, Jonah's included. The head/shaft ratio of any of them... I had no idea.

"His is perfect, not too big, not too small."

"Great," Laura said dryly. "The Berenstain Bears of penises."

"Not Berenstain Bears," Ling interjected. "Three Little Pigs."

"ANYWAY," Chelsea continued. "It's also rugged. Like, that seems like a weird word to describe a cock, but it's so utterly masculine. He dropped his pants, and I swear to God, I wanted to just drop to my knees and worship it."

Laura, whose bitchiness levels rivaled her devotion to Jesus, paled at the false Gods picture that Chelsea was painting. I chewed on a forkful of salad and theorized that Chelsea had probably already been on her knees at that point.

"And it's big, obviously," Chelsea carried on, unaware that conversations on both sides of our trio had stopped as the legend of Easton grew. *Pun intended.* She dropped her fork with a clink against the bowl and held out her palms, spreading them a sizable distance apart until even Laura hissed with approval.

"But honestly," Chelsea continued airily, dropping her hands and plucking a crouton out of her salad. "It wasn't that it was big, or beautiful, that really mattered. What mattered..." she paused for effect.

The cliffhanger worked on all of us, including me. I eyed the clock at the end of the room, aware that I should have left three minutes ago. Stuffing another mouthful of salad into my mouth, I chewed faster and waited for Chelsea's next words.

"What mattered," she repeated, leaning forward as if she was about to deliver the Holy Grail of gossip. "Was how he used it."

"Used his penis?" Ling asked stupidly, and for someone with the highest GPA in our pledge class, she was painfully dumb at times.

"Yes, Ling. His *penis*." Laura puffed out her cheeks and made a big show of picking up her Louis Vuitton satchel and sliding it over one shoulder. "Well, this was fun. Chelsea slept with someone else. Whoop Dee Do. I'll spread the word."

I saw, in the brief moment when Chelsea's eyebrows knitted together, the pain of the impact. The evidence cleared quickly and she laughed, meeting my eyes without responding to Laura.

"Prude," I muttered as soon as the Lilly Pulitzer-clad brunette was out of earshot.

"Right?" Chelsea tucked the long part of her bangs behind her ear. "Anyways, it was amazing. Like, four orgasms amazing. I don't know how I'll find anyone to compare with it."

"Maybe you won't have to," Ling suggested. "Maybe you will get married and have babies and screw like bunnies until you're old and wrinkly." She giggled at us over the edge of her thick calculus textbook and I really loved her in that moment, despite her naiveté. Because the rest of us knew that Easton wouldn't marry Chelsea. In the rules of college life, the male slut never marries the female slut. The male slut finds a good girl, someone untainted and naive, and moves her to the suburbs where he gives her 2.5 orgasms, three times a week, along with the shopping list.

He would marry me, but Chelsea and Ling and bitchy Laura and I didn't realize that yet. All we knew was that Easton North had a nice cock. And that simple fact was what, years later, got me into this mess.

On my knees, between two men. My husband's hand on the back of my head.

2

There was something in the air that night. A breathless anticipation. I felt it when I was getting ready, my hand hovering over the plain cotton panties before selecting the silk thong. I embraced it when I sidled up to the bar, my fake id pushed forward with brazen confidence, and ordered tequila shots instead of beers.

It was three weeks before summer and we were restless, our thoughts warring between tan lines and exam dates, each weekend embraced with reckless abandon in anticipation of the slow summer ahead. Chelsea, four guys past Easton North, was going to chase a surfer up to Jersey for the summer. Laura had an internship at the Junior League of St Pete, and Ling would be studying abroad in Korea. I'd be the only one staying, my ice cream scooping gig paying the rent as I shuffled through two summer semesters that would knock out twelve easy credits.

I liked the summers, liked the ability to find a parking spot without divine intervention, liked the easy familiarity that I found in my classmates, liked the house parties that weren't packed to the vents with freshmen. But still, I felt the desperation like everyone else. The countdown before the year ended. The primal need for one last human connection before they were all gone.

I could have counted down to the moment Chelsea vomited with freakish accuracy. All of the elements were there. Beer, then liquor. *Never been sicker.* Tequila followed by rum. *Not so much fun.* When she climbed onto the bar, her thick cork wedges crunching over a finger along the way, I braced for it. When she hung upside down from the glass rack, I winced. When she stumbled from the bar top and toward the bathroom, I steered her to the closest bush and still didn't get her there in time.

I watched the brown liquid splash precariously close to my new Steve Maddens and listened to the chant of a hundred drunk girls to Brown Eyed Girl's chorus.

"I'm fine," she croaked, though no one was really asking.

"Come on." I tugged her upright and looked around for something to wipe off her chin with. "Stay right here. I'm going to get you a napkin."

She wobbled to the right and I carefully settled her into one of the bar's wrought iron chairs. "Stay," I instructed.

I turned to head to the bar and ran into him. "Sorry," I murmured, moving right.

"Here."

It was just a word. Four letters. Innocent ones, but like Chelsea's whispered curse in the middle of the sorority dining hall, they caught my attention in an instant. I looked up, and that was my mistake.

Gorgeous trouble, that's what he looked like. The innocent kind that wore polos and khakis to church on Sunday, then fucked you on their family's yacht. The messy hair, Master's baseball cap, strong jaw, and blue-eyed prom king kind. The sort that would toss someone like Jonah aside and fling a girl over his shoulder and spank her ass.

Not that I was thinking about Jonah right then. After the last weekend, I wasn't thinking about Jonah *ever* again. Ironically, that mental vow brought to mind the image of him, his tongue halfway down *her* throat, his hand squeezing her push-up bra boob. Thank God we'd decided to go out. Thank God I'd gone up to the upper deck. Thank God I'd seen them, before my heart had really fallen for him.

"Here." The guy's hand moved and I focused in on the chunk of paper towels he held out.

"Oh. Wow. Thanks." A 4.0 average and I was sputtering out syllables like a toddler.

"I'll do it." He pulled the napkins out of reach and crouched beside Chelsea, carefully wiping the thick cord of vomit off her chin. I winced at her non-reaction, her eyes on me, one hand swinging through the air toward me. "Let's dance!" she cried out.

Let's not. I watched as he tapped at her knee, bringing her attention to him. "Chelsea? Let's get you home. Come on. I'll take you."

My surprise at his recognition of her was trumped by the alarming thought of her leaving with him. "No." I worked my way in between them and hoisted her limp arm over my shoulder, struggling to pull her to her feet. "I've got her."

"Oh my GAWD," Chelsea sang out, completely oblivious to the horrible breath she was blasting in our direction. "You guys are fighting over me! This is so cute."

The guy chuckled, a flash of white teeth showing, and discreetly tossed the dirty napkin in the closest black bagged trash can. "Adorable," he agreed, taking her other arm and slinging it around his shoulder.

He lifted her with ease, getting her through the exit gate and onto the sidewalk as I stumbled behind them, trying to keep up while he hefted a sizable amount of drunk Chelsea.

"Wait," I protested. "Stop."

He stopped, Chelsea kept going, and we both lunged to keep her upright.

"I should probably just carry her," he offered.

"He is sooo strong," Chelsea agreed.

"I appreciate your help, but I've got it from here." I fished in my back pocket for my phone. "I'll call a cab. We'll be fine."

He glanced down the dark street, then back toward the loud bar. A belch sounded from somewhere, followed by the thump of a cheap car radio. "I don't feel right leaving you alone."

"Elle, E's a gentleman!" Chelsea squawked.

"My car's right there. I'll drive you to the sorority house." He nodded toward a dark parking lot that looked like the perfect place to chop someone's head off, assuming you wanted to use a late model BMW as the chopping block. "I'm sober," he added.

"A SOBER gentleman!" Chelsea amended, her volume raising an octave past bearable.

"Look." He reached into his back pocket and took out his wallet, pulled out his driver's license and held it out to me. "Take a picture. Text it to a friend."

I took the ID from him and made a show of looking between the image and him. Dayum. Baseball cap off, he was even hotter. My thumb moved, exposing his name. *Easton North.* I inhaled without thinking, my drunken state not too far gone to forget the lunchroom conversation that had scarred poor Ling for weeks. How had Chelsea described his dick? *Pretty.* But also, something else. *Rugged?* Had that been it?

I could feel my cheeks burn as I unlocked my phone and took a photo, one I quickly texted to Ling along with a dozen exclamation points and a text that would probably confuse her.

This guy is driving me and Chelsea home. If we disappear, tell them we died of a rugged cock.

I started to laugh, sent the text, then handed him the license.

"What?" He looked at the card as if there was something wrong with it.

My giggles broke the dam into full-blown laughter.

"What?" He repeated, a slow smile spreading over that

gorgeous face as if he was fighting the urge to join in. "Is it my age? Too old for you?"

I rolled my eyes and gestured toward Chelsea, indicating that he could go ahead and pick her up. "It's not your age." I fought the urge to pull my phone back out and examine the birthdate on the photo. Was he younger than us? Older? Maybe he was ancient, one of these twenty-eight-year-old college kids that had stretched four years into ten. He lifted Chelsea up and she swooped, her hands lifting into the air as if she was on a ride. I eyed her closely and hoped she was done vomiting.

"My height?" He guessed, nodding towards a white sedan at the edge of the lot. "That's mine."

"I've been in this car," Chelsea said loudly, as the car's headlights flashed.

"It wasn't your height." It was a nice height. Totally uncomical.

I opened the back seat and held the door open, watching critically as he carefully maneuvered her into the space.

"By *been in this car*," she stage whispered, "I meant in the biblical sense."

Easton shot me an apologetic look and I bit my bottom lip to keep from laughing again.

"We were dru—" he started to say, and she cut him off with an earsplitting yell.

"We are IN LOVE Easton North. Don't you dare diminish the beauty that it is!"

I raised my brows at him, letting him sweat for an excruciatingly entertaining moment as he carefully moved her feet into the car and shut the door. From inside, Chelsea began to belt out the national anthem.

"Well," he said quietly, spinning his car key around one finger. "I don't know how well you know Chelsea, but we are, in fact, betrothed to be married."

I think it was at that moment that I fell for him. Right then, in my beer-stained J Crew capris, with Chelsea singing the Star-Spangled Banner at the top of her lungs, in the night that was still soaked in anticipation.

"I did know," I said with a quiet smile. "I'm actually your maid of honor."

"Ahhh…" he said. "So you're the tempting maid of honor with the bedroom eyes and bachelorette antics. I've been warned about you." He opened the passenger car door and waited for me to get in. "You're the one who's going to seduce me on my wedding night and whisk me away to your dungeon of passion."

I let out a laugh as I stepped into the car. I hadn't expected the fabled Easton North to be charming. Pulling the seatbelt over my chest, I tried to place the reason Chelsea stopped seeing him. Had it been her decision or his? I don't think there had even been a decision, actually. I think, like so many of her relationships, they had hooked up a few times, then wandered away. Case in point— tonight, which had been a calculated attempt for her to seduce Tainted Love's guitarist, only the band had canceled last minute and left us with a DJ who seemed to have last year's hit list on repeat.

He made sure my feet were inside, then shut the door. I looked through the dusty windshield at Potbelly's, the bar still over-flowing with drunk bodies who didn't care what was pumping through the speakers.

He sat down in the driver's seat and inserted the key, the engine whining as it sputtered, then came to life. I carefully moved my heels out of the way of a pile of empty Gatorade bottles in his floorboard. Definitely not the sleek Challenger that Jonah vacu-umed out and waxed every Sunday afternoon.

"So, Ellen? Is that right?"

Technically it was, but I'd crawl under my comforter and die before responding to that. "Elle." I studied the bar. "Do you have friends you need to say goodbye to?"

"Nah, I'll come back after I drop you guys off." He put the car in reverse and turned toward me, gripping the back of my seat as he looked behind him and backed the car up. I shifted closer to the door and tried not to notice the way the edge of his thumb touched my shoulder. From the backseat, Chelsea mumbled through a horrific rendition of the anthem's third verse, unbothered by the conflicting song playing through Easton's speakers.

"So, what about you?" He braked and looked at me, the dim lighting in the car only enhancing his features.

"What about me?"

"Are you betrothed?"

I smiled. "You know nobody says betrothed."

He gave me a mock puzzled look. "Every guy on the baseball team says betrothed. Like, every day. It's second in line to glove."

I rolled my eyes. "Okay."

"That was my humble segue into mentioning I'm on the baseball team." He pulled to the edge of the lot and glanced right, before turning left. I tried not to be bothered by the fact that he knew exactly where our sorority house was.

"Very suave," I remarked. "And well needed. With a name like Easton, I assumed you were a tuba player."

It was his turn to laugh, and a shot of pleasure hit at the unrestrained sound that came from him. He glanced at me, amused, and I fought to keep my features bored. "So?" he asked. "Are you in love?"

"That's an odd question," I shifted in my seat and watched the approaching light turn red. We slowed to a stop, and a trio of guys stepped into the road. "Most guys just ask if I'm dating anyone."

"Most guys are probably hitting on you."

"Which you aren't," I said skeptically.

"I'm just asking a question." He smiled as if he knew exactly how devastating the impact was.

"She's single," Chelsea crowed. "Very very VERY single."

I groaned and turned to glare at my best friend. "I'm not *that* single."

"You should date E," she announced brightly, as if she had just had the idea of a lifetime. "You guys would be perfect together!"

Easton gasped as if offended. "I thought we were in love. What happened to diminishing our beauty and all of that?"

"Yeah, yeah, yeah," she rattled off. "You guys can diminish your own beauty."

He turned down our street, the short ride almost painful in its quick trajectory. "ADPi, right? You want me to drop you off in front or back?"

"The front please." I found my clutch on the floorboard and turned to Chelsea, holding on to the seat as he drove across the pothole just before our house. "We're at the house. Please be quiet."

She snorted in response. I unclipped my seatbelt. "Thanks for the ride. I'll get her in."

"Wait." He grabbed my hand and the contact felt too intimate. "I never found out why you laughed at my license."

I scrunched up my nose. "Maybe I'll tell you next time I see you." I pulled my hand free and cranked open the door. "If I see you." Stepping out, I waited for Chelsea, getting a full view of her panties as she hoisted herself out of the backseat with an unlady-like burp.

"Thanks, E." She leaned back in the car and waved her fingers at him like she was casting a spell. "I'll text you Elle's phone number later."

"No, SHE WON'T," I said loudly.

Chelsea laughed as she swung the door shut and turned to me, wrapping one arm around my shoulders in a fierce hug. "I did that for you, you know. The whole vomit thing. It was to get you two together."

"Likely." I struggled under her weight and aimed us toward the stately southern mansion's front door. "But you did it very well. The vomiting was perfectly executed."

"I thought so," she said modestly. "I've been practicing."

I planted an affectionate kiss on her blonde curls and left her side, getting to the door first and punching in our passcode, holding my finger to my mouth to indicate that she should stay quiet. It was after curfew, so house noise was required to be at a minimum. We tiptoed in and waved silently to a cluster of girls in the den, under blankets, with the television quietly playing. Moving down the wood hall, we headed to the open sleeping porches at the back of the house, the beds reserved for any sister who needed a place to crash after too much studying or partying.

"Goodnight." Chelsea fell, face-first, on the closest bed. I carefully extracted her phone from her back pocket, plugged it in beside her, and patted the top of her head.

"Night."

3

Summer came and Easton North stayed, like a final Girl Scout cookie you keep in the box, debating over the right time to finally pull it out and eat it. I wanted to eat him. God, I wanted to pounce on that tall athletic frame and wrestle him to the ground. Devour that adorable smirk.

But I didn't. Out of a misplaced respect for Chelsea, who was tits deep in Jersey trash, and a wariness of all men after Jonah's betrayal—I stayed as far away from Easton North as I could. During the school year, it would have been easy. Thirty thousand bodies allowed for easy avoidance, which is how I didn't know about Jonah's hookups until three months into our relationship. But in the summer, campus became a smaller place. Faces became familiar. Parties were more intimate. The inevitable bump of Easton and me happened, again and again, like discarded rafts along a shore.

A house party. Red solo cups in hand, chants filling the air, a chug-off in progress, my hip collided with his. I turned to apologize, then saw Easton and laughed. He moved closer, and I stepped away. "We're just leaving!" I called out, over a Bone Thugs song just ancient enough to be cool. Turning my head, I looked for my roommate as proof I wasn't alone.

He made a face and lifted his cup, draining the contents, his eyes staying on me. The baseball hat was still present, but turned around, tufts of hair sticking out from its clip, his light blue eyes on full display. "I know why you laughed!" he called as I went to escape, my flip flops clipping toward the door.

I glanced back and paused.

He lifted the empty cup and crooked his top finger, beckoning me closer. Such a player. So much confidence in that cocky smile. He knew I'd come. Knew I'd let him lean in and whisper whatever bullshit he was about to say. He knew that no girl could resist those bedroom eyes and perfect build.

By some Herculean feat of will, I turned and left, squeezing through the crowd, my hand tightening on my cup as some of the warm Coors Light splashed out. I left and, sadly enough, Easton North didn't follow.

The library. My pencil jittered along the page, 10mg of Adderall doing their job as I scribbled notes at a furious pace. The chair next to me creaked into motion, its feet wheezing along the carpet as someone pulled it out.

I finished the section and set down my pencil, reading over my notes and attempting to memorize the rules of binomial distribution. Closing my eyes, I moved through the steps in my mind, trying to picture each line in the textbook.

Something light tapped at my pinky fingers, and I opened my eyes and stared down at my hand.

It was a ripped piece of paper, folded in half. A note. I glanced to my right and saw him there, a worn green Jansport beside an open composition pad, his eyes crinkled at the edges with humor. His gaze dropped to the note and mine followed suit. I unfolded the paper and squinted at the cramped but neat handwriting in blue ink.

Tell me why you laughed and I'll leave you alone.

There was a line drawn below the promise, a blank waiting to be filled. I let out a dramatic and exasperated sigh and leaned forward, using my pencil to fill in the blank.

I thought you knew.

I pushed it toward him, face up on the table. He leaned over, read the response, and the faint scent of soap wafted over. His hair was wet and thick, shaggy over his forehead, and I wondered where his baseball cap was.

His gaze flicked to me and the corner of his mouth twitched. Chelsea once told me that his mouth was magic. She hadn't been talking about a kiss. She'd described, in enough explicit detail to fill a Penthouse Forum, exactly how Easton North had gone down on her. I'd tried not to think about those details for the last four weeks. Tried, while watching a slow smile tug across his lips, to not let my mind wander back through her story.

He hunched over the pad and wrote something else, then carefully bent the page and tore it in half, folding it into quarters and sliding it across the worn wooden surface toward me. It came to a stop six inches from my hand which, according to legend, was three inches shorter than his dick.

I made a big show of glancing at my watch and then, in a bored and annoyed fashion, picked up the note and spread it out on the table. I think my mouth cheated. I could feel the smile tugging at my cheeks in anticipation of what it would say.

You know I don't know.

My pencil moved on its own accord.

It was about your dick.

I stared at the line, unsure if I actually wanted to light this fire.

I couldn't just say that and leave. There would be another conversation. He'd chase. Ask questions. It would be an intentional act to pull him toward me.

I balled the note into the tiniest piece I could manage and set it on the desk. Forming a circle with my thumb and my forefinger, I flicked the edge of it and watched it sail through the air and land on the other side of the room, behind two rows of tables. He stared in the direction it had disappeared, then looked back at me. I stretched, letting my back bend over the lip of the chair, then stood, gathering my books.

"Have a good night," I whispered and gave him an innocent smile. Taking my time, I meandered slowly around the edge of the bookshelves. As soon as I cleared the corner and out of his sight, I started to run away.

The club. The guy before me was straight South Florida, all spiked gel hair and that *hey mama* game that worked great on Delta Gammas but fell flat on me. I glanced over his shoulder, searching the crowd for Lizzy, who was my summer stand-in for Chelsea. A little taller, a lot sweeter, but without the crude honesty I'd grown to love in my slutty best friend.

"It's fate, us meeting again." The Miami boy leaned against the high top, his pelvis trapping me against my stool. "The gym and now here?"

That wasn't fate. This club was the only place to be on a Tuesday night, and half the campus had a workout addiction. I could turn in a circle and point out ten people I'd seen in the gym in the last week. The only person I hadn't seen—not that I'd been looking—was Easton, thanks to the private gym that campus athletes used. Either way, I was two weeks out from our late-night library encounter and had avoided him thus far.

"I know," I managed a smile. "Crazy."

"What's your major?" His eyes bored into mine, and it wasn't terrible to have the attention, even if it was unoriginal in nature. If *what's your sign?* was the pickup line of the 90's, *what's your major* was the standard go-to when two students had shit in common.

"Philosophy."

He nodded as if my response meant something. Hell, I was three years in, and I didn't really know what a degree in Philosophy prepared anyone for. It didn't matter. Undergrad was a skipping stone I had to jump in order to get to law school, and communications, according to my advisor, was my best shot at a class rank and GPA that would impress the law school admissions board.

"You?" I lifted the heavy wave of hair off my back and fanned my face.

"Real Estate." He flashed a grin at me, as if I should be impressed. "My family is in development. You know Clearingworth?"

I stared at him blankly and he scoffed, then recovered. "It's seriously the biggest retirement community in Boyton. It's got over—"

He said more, but I didn't hear it. I saw his animated movements, felt the heat of him as he leaned closer, yelling to be heard over the music. I felt his hand settle on my hip but ignored it all as I focused in on Easton.

His head was bobbing to the music, his attention on the woman before him. I glanced briefly at the blonde, then back at him, catching his profile as he lifted his drink, then held the cup out of her way.

"It's legit. I can show it to you." His diamond stud earring moved left and blocked my view. I didn't even know this guy's name.

"Let's dance." I clamped my hand around his wrist and dragged him toward the floor, ignoring his protests as I set up shop a few couples over from Easton.

"Whoa, mamacita." He sipped his drink with the tiny straw and pulled me closer, pinning me against his body. "That's what I'm talking about."

I knew what I was doing when I started to dance with him. His hand slid down the back of my dress and gripped my ass and I let him. His tongue, cold from the drink, dipped into my mouth. I pulled back and his fingers tightened, pulling me into his pelvis and I dared a glance over one shoulder and found Easton in the crowd, his eyes on me. For once, there wasn't an ounce of playfulness in their depths.

I escaped from my Latin lover halfway into the next song and squeezed through the crowd, heading for the dim hall that led to the bathrooms. Just before the break of bodies, a hand clamped around my wrist, pulling me right and into an empty nook, just behind the stage speakers.

"What the fuck are you doing?" Easton was close, pushing me back against the wall, his voice a growl in my ear, his body flush against mine.

"What?" I gave a half-hearted attempt to push against his chest. "What are you talking about?"

"Is that what you like?" His hands settled on my waist and he pulled me tighter against him. He jerked his head toward the crowd. "Rico Suave types?"

"Maybe." I leaned my shoulders back against the wall and looked up at him. "Does it matter?"

"Yeah," he said quietly. "It matters."

"Why?"

He started to say something and stopped, changing course. "Why do you keep running from me?"

"I've got to go to the bathroom." I pushed off the wall and stood.

His hands tightened, holding me in place. "Uh-uh," he said darkly. "You're not running from me again."

"I have to pee," I said, clearly enunciating every unsexy syllable.

That smile cracked along his face. "You don't have to pee."

"I do," I insisted.

"You went to the bathroom fifteen minutes ago and haven't drank anything since. You either have a bladder infection or you're too chicken to talk to me."

"I—" My mouth opened, then shut.

"Which is it, Elle? Horrific infection or intimated by my sexual prowess?" He cocked one brow, waiting. As if I could choose either of those paths.

I crossed my arms over my chest. "Maybe I just don't like you. Ever thought of that?"

He chuckled and leaned closer until his mouth was at my ear. "If you didn't like me, you wouldn't have kissed him."

"Oh my God," I sputtered. "That's the stupidest—" I pushed against his chest and he stayed in place, my palms now resting on the strong planes of his pecs.

"It worked." He lifted his head away from my ear and met my gaze, his mouth less than a foot from mine. "I saw you kiss him and wanted to rip him in two."

I needed to stop looking into his eyes. Needed to stop clinging to his shirt. Needed to stop my body from leaning into his heat.

"You have no idea of the things I want to do to you," he growled, his gaze dropping to my mouth, his fingers tightening on my hips. He lowered his mouth and I tried to stay still, tried not to meet his lips halfway.

I tried, and I failed. Pushing off the wall, I collided into his mouth.

Four hours later, in a tiny apartment overlooking the stadium, I met the beauty that was Easton's cock.

Chelsea was right. It was pretty. It was perfect. It overwhelmed my pleasure receptors and unleashed a sexual monster inside me. A monster that, seven years later, would start to eat away at our lives.

4

3 years later

EASTON

Florida State had been full of women. It was started as a women's college, back in the 70's, and the demographic remained slanted, pussy spilling across this campus in every direction but up.

I came down on a recruiting trip in March. Left my house with a scarf and gloves, and boarded a 747 that sat on the runway for an extra forty-five minutes to allow a blizzard to pass.

Six hours later, I was on a bus, rolling through palm trees and looking at girls in bikinis, stretched out like hot dogs on a broiler, outside their dorm.

I'd signed my letter of intent the next morning, and started envisioning my college career at Florida State. Pitching no-hitters to the sound of cheers. Beer flowing like water. A different brunette in my bed every night. A suntan in December. Leaving

Tallahassee with a big check in hand and pro contract, untethered and on the top of the world.

I hadn't expected Elle. I'd kissed her and immediately felt my plans shift, my future realigning, my dreams diluting as she came into sharp focus.

"Fuck me." She looked up from her spot on the stained oak floor and blew a breath upward, her dark hair blowing out of her eyes. "You won't believe this, but I think we put this on backward." She held out the instruction package, her finger pinned on a diagram, her massive wedding ring flashing under the chandelier's delicate light. "Look at the feet. Ours are facing left."

I studied the diagram, comparing the cramped image with the maze of pieces laid out on the floor before Elle. "These are the screws we just put in?"

"Yeah. All of them." She groaned and leaned back on her hands, tilting her head back at an angle that exposed her throat. God, I loved that throat. Loved feeling the pulse of her heartbeat as I kissed down its length. Loved the flex of its muscles as she took me down its gullet. Loved the stiffening of it when she got mad. "Maybe we should run up and get that bit."

The fourteen screws that held the IKEA dresser's back piece on were all some sort of eight-sided Allen wrench that we didn't have a drill bit for. The dresser's instruction package had included a wrench for manual tightening and it had taken almost twenty minutes for us to affix the screws to the wrong side of the teal board. She'd chosen the dresser for its color, the blue shade almost a perfect match for the uniforms that hung in my closet.

"Almost straight to the pros," my agent had crowed. *"Do you know what this means? They have big plans for you, Easton. Big plans. Settle into Miami. You're going to own this town."*

I'd believed him, my faith confirmed by the million-dollar contract. I'd believed him when we'd bought this house. When we'd charged my new American Express card with almost forty-thousand dollars of furniture. When I'd put my beautiful wife behind the wheel of a new BMW.

Big plans for me. *Right.* I tossed the instructions down and held out my hand to help her up. "Yeah, let's go."

"And while we're out, maybe we can get ice cream." She pulled on my hand and my vision spun for a moment.

I steadied myself and glanced at my watch. "We better hurry if we're going to get there before they close."

She looked down at the clusterfuck of pieces, laid out like a jigsaw across our master bedroom floor. We were almost four hours into the assembly, our progress interrupted by sex, then a check-the-mail and social media break, then a walk to the neighbor's house to return the dolly we'd borrowed. "It'll be quick once we have the drill bit."

"Super quick. We can knock it when we get back."

"Maybe we should just do it tomorrow. Fresh minds and all." She grinned at me and I was so fucking lucky this woman loved me.

I forced a smile. "Tomorrow sounds like a good idea."

"What time do you have to be at the field?"

I reached into my pocket, checking for my keys and wallet. "They're giving me tomorrow off."

"Really?" She brushed the front of her pants off. "For your concussion? I thought you still had to be at practice."

A lie sat at the tip of my tongue, heavy and wet. I watched the way she stepped carefully over the dismantled dresser and ached at the thought of losing her.

What would she say when she found out? How would she feel? Would she have the same crushing fears that I had? Would she look around this huge new house and that diamond on her finger, and see it all as a mistake?

I'd been afraid of her since the first time she laughed at me. Instantly addicted to that smile, instantly wary of what my chemical and mental attraction to her meant. I'd found it and lost, then gave into it and was—in a sense—found. And she'd been the very first thing I thought about when the X-ray was lit.

The very first thing when the doctor called Coach Wade into the room.

The very first thing when I placed the call to my agent, desperate for a reassurance that everything wasn't lost.

But it was. I'd been in baseball since I was seven. I'd studied the greats. Inhaled ESPN. Knew the long list that could instantly kill a career.

For a pitcher, a skull fracture was lethal.

"Hey." She stopped in front of me and smoothed down the front of my shirt, her fingers outlining the muscles in my chest. "You okay?"

I swallowed. "I need to tell you something."

She paused, and her gaze snapped from my chin to my eyes. "Okay," she said cautiously.

I loved every expression she gave but that look. That apprehensive linger of her eyes. The fear behind them. The pinch of her brows and flattening of her lips. She'd bristled in the same fashion when she'd slid the receipt across the table at Red Lobster, the waitress's number in bubbly print across the bottom of it. I'd seen the tightening of her hands on her purse, the idea of flight in her eyes. It hadn't been my doing, and it wasn't the first waitress who tried to give me her number, but it had scared the absolute shit out of Elle.

My brave woman grew shell-shocked in certain situations. Instability was a trigger, and I'd spent the last three years trying to show her how fucking much I loved her. How I would never leave her. How I would never cheat, or do anything to risk our marriage, or her happiness.

Big words, considering that I was about to rip her world in two.

"It's not just a concussion." I rolled my neck without thinking, and my head throbbed. "They went over the x-rays with me today."

"Okay." She sat next to me on the couch under the back porch, her jeans tickling the hairs on my leg. "So what is it?"

"A skull fracture." I blew out a hard breath. "It's bad, Elle. Career-ending."

"Are you in pain?"

"Not really." I gently touched the side of my head, running my finger over the knot where the line drive had connected with my skull. I never saw it coming. I pitched the ball, then woke up on the table, the team doc peering down at me. It had been an away game, and Elle had watched it happen in high-definition, then left a dozen tearful messages on my cell before getting a hold of me.

"Is it dangerous? Are there long-term side effects? I looked up skull fractures that night, and it said—"

"The doc says I'm good, but the risk is too high for me to ever play again. Another line drive could kill me."

She inhaled sharply. "E."

She hadn't heard the worst, and I steeled myself as I delivered the news. "And the contract renewal hasn't been signed. We sent it back to them with some markups." Stupid fucking markups. Use of owner's plane and private suite, a six-figure bonus when I won the Cy Young. If I had just signed the contract, I'd have a seven-year deal with a guaranteed $12M payout. It wouldn't matter if I tripped on a curb and shattered my femur, or if I lobbed peaches over the plate. *Guaranteed* money. We'd have been set and the jagged crack along my skull wouldn't have mattered.

Her hand tightened on mine. "Don't worry about that. Can you do a different position? One that doesn't run a risk of line drives?"

"They cut me. I was my pitch. That's it."

Her eyes closed for one, long painful moment. When they opened again, I watched a tear run down her cheek, quick and frantic, as if it was racing to get offscreen before it was seen. I caught it with my finger and wiped it away.

Three years together, and she's cried four times. Once, at the movies. Once, locked with me in a small bathroom at Wakulla Springs. Once, the night I proposed. And last week, her voicemails drenched in worried tears.

At Wakulla Springs, I swore to myself I'd do anything I could to keep her from crying in sadness again. I'd failed.

She met my eyes and my gut twisted at the heartache in her dark brown eyes. "I'm sorry," she whispered. "I'm so sorry."

"I'm sorry." I balled my hand into a fist. "I shouldn't have asked for anything. I should have signed that contract and—"

"I'm not talking about the money, E." She looked down at my fists, and gently opened them with her hands. Another tear dripped down her cheek and I let it fall, then felt like a failure. An even bigger failure. "You love it so much," she whispered, her voice thick. "I can't imagine losing that." She looked up at me, and we were on two completely different planets.

"The house," I managed. "The money. I don't even know what we fucking have left." *Three hundred grand? Two?* After my agent cut and taxes... I glanced into the yard and thought of the deposit I'd put down on the six-figure pool renovation. We were going to add in a hot tub. Waterfall. A slide for our future kids. We were going to sip champagne in the shallow end and fuck in the hot tub. We'd have to back out and lose that deposit.

"Ignore the money," she said sharply. "We fell in love in shit apartments drinking Natty Light and six-dollar fried chicken. We took a Greyhound to Panama City for a romantic weekend." She waved a hand behind her. "We can sell the house. We can get real jobs and be normal." She cupped my face, the tips of her short nails scratching along my scruff. "We're going to have beautiful babies and teach them your sense of humor and my intelligence, and be so fucking happy, E. I can give you that. But I can't give you baseball and I'm so sorry about that."

"I can't think about that right now." My hands tightened on her waist. "And you don't deserve Greyhounds and Natty Light. You deserve everything and I was supposed to give it to you."

"You did." She leaned forward and kissed me. "And I love you for it, but all I need is you. And I'm worried you need baseball to be happy."

"I don't," I said hoarsely. "I just need to know that you won't leave me." I couldn't do life without her. Baseball, yes. But not her.

She moved into my lap and curled against my chest, wrapping her arms around my bicep and hugging it tightly. "I will *never* leave you," she promised fiercely. "Never."

My tension broke at her words, given without hesitation. I pressed a kiss against her head and fought back my own tears, my emotions warring with the deep sadness her concerns brought.

Because she was right. She couldn't give me baseball—and I didn't know who I was without it.

5

4 years later - present

ELLE

There are things they don't tell you about marriage. LOTS of things.

I watched my parents sail into a thirty-year anniversary without a single fight. Occasionally there would be tension. Some painfully quiet dinners. An irritated huff from my father when my mother would turn off the television in the middle of his game. But no fights, certainly none like this.

The egg salad, which I had wasted forty minutes on and looked nothing like Rachel Ray's, sailed through the kitchen and splattered against our pale green cabinets, completely missing their target. I grunted, turned back to the fridge and grabbed the first thing my hand came in contact with—the tub of sour cream. Whirling on one foot, I ripped off the lid and flung the container in the direction of my husband, the tub landing face first square in the middle of his crisp blue dress shirt.

Silence fell.

He dropped his chin and watched as the tub sagged, slowly easing down the neat line of buttons, a sticky white mess of cream in its wake. It fell to the floor with a loud splat. He growled and lunged toward me, tripping over our Great Dane, who skittered left then right, torn between getting out of the way and defending my honor. I grabbed the carton of eggs from the fridge door and ran.

"ONE CARD!" I screamed as I made it to the dining room and turned, heaving the carton toward him. He reached out, catching the foam container one-handed. If he'd had such quick reflexes four years ago, maybe he wouldn't have caught that line drive with his temple. "ONE CARD!"

I made it to the slider door and flipped the latch, tugging at the handle and trying to get the stubborn door down its track. God, I hated this house. Why had I bought into his stupid ideas of charm and character? We could be in a fucking McMansion for the price we'd paid. I could have hot water every evening, an air conditioner that didn't rattle like a steam kettle, and real closets, the sort with roll-out drawers and lighting and electrical outlets that didn't spark when you plugged into them.

In four giant steps, he was at my side, his hand hard against the door jam, keeping it in place. "I'm sorry about the card. I didn't realize what a big deal it was to you."

"It's not a big deal," I said hotly, avoiding his eye contact as I pinned my lips together. "It's just that I told you this last year, and you should have remembered. I shouldn't HAVE to tell you. If I tell you to get me a card, then it loses the ENTIRE *FUCKING* POINT OF THE CARD!"

I was screaming again. Why was I screaming? I shouldn't be this emotional. If my mother was here, she'd have her shrink glasses on, her prescription tablet out, judgment all over that botox-enhanced face. *The depth of your emotion mimics the depth of your feelings, Ellen. Release your emotions to release those feelings.* THAT was a line of fresh pig shit. I'd released lots of emotions in the last fifteen minutes and I was still mad as hell over the slight.

"Elle, I'm sorry. Please forgive me."

I watched him warily, knowing my husband too well to be fooled by this passive response.

"I am so *so* sorry that I didn't get you a card for Mother's Day." He looked sincere, but I could see the exasperation in those baby blues. "But babe—"

"Don't you fucking say it," I warned.

"He's—"

"Don't you say it!"

"He's a fucking dog." He gestured to the hundred-and-forty-pound beast behind him. "And he's not a very good one."

This wasn't about Wayland. How did he not understand that? I ducked under his arm and made for the hall, my right hip colliding sharply with the corner of the table. I swore and swung out, my forward progress thwarted by the iron grip he clamped on the back of my shirt.

"Hey!" I twisted, clawing behind me. "You're messing up my shirt!"

"Fuck the shirt," he growled, yanking at the thin fabric until I was in his reach, his arms wrapping around my torso, his body pinning me against my mother's hand-painted dining dresser. "Look at me."

I didn't. I couldn't. I stared stubbornly at the sliding glass door and cursed it for sticking. If it had only opened, I'd be outside right now. I'd be running. Wayland would have lunged for the door, Easton would have gone for Wayland, and I could have escaped in the confusion of the moment.

"Elle," he said quietly. "Look at me."

I risked everything and flipped my eyes to his for one tiny moment.

He had such beautiful eyes. Pale blue. Baby blue. The same

color I would have painted the upstairs nursery. I even had a paint color, one picked from the rainbow of samples, with Easton's eyes in mind. Now, they studied me with the same cautious intensity they'd carried on our wedding day, when he asked if I was sure I wanted to marry him.

"You aren't supposed to ask that," I replied, pulling at the sleeve of my bathrobe, the material itchy despite the spa's assurances that it was polyester free. "You aren't even supposed to be here. It's bad luck."

"I just want to make sure. This is for life. Are you sure that I'm the man you want to spend forever with?" He caged me in, his hands on each shoulder, and peered at me as if trying to see the image in a Magic Eye puzzle.

"Of course I'm sure," I laughed. "I love you."

I'd been so confident. So unconcerned. I'd kissed my future husband and shooed him away from the dressing area. I hadn't stopped to ask why he was asking the question, or taken a moment to really analyze my answer.

Maybe he should have asked himself that question. Maybe if he had, he'd be celebrating Mother's Day with a bundle of coo-worthy toddlers, and not a giant dog and overly-emotional wife.

"I'm sorry that I didn't get you a card," he said, smoothing my hair away from my face. "I'm going to go, right now, and fix that. And I'll never forget again, I promise."

He shouldn't have forgotten this year. Last year I said something about it. Something small, a flippant comment that had sailed past ESPN and gotten lost in our living room curtains. I'd waited until Sports Center was over and then went upstairs to draw a bath. Sitting in the tepid water, I cursed our faulty hot water heater and sobbed my emotions out. This year, I hadn't had the self-control and couldn't face the idea of another failed Mother's Day. Another holiday of waiting expectantly for something that may never come.

"Is this about..." he hesitated.

Yes. Of course it was. The Unnameable. The EPT test box, flattened and turned inside out, stuffed at the bottom of the trash can so he wouldn't see. The subtle seductions between the fourteenth and sixteenth day of my cycle. The prenatal vitamins that I dumped into the women's multivitamin, just so I didn't have to see the happy pregnant woman on the bottle.

"No." I was trying for a breezy tone, but the word croaked out of me. "It's not. It's just that I didn't want that damn dog to begin with—" I lowered my voice to spare Wayland's feelings— "and *I'm* the one who cleans up his torn pillows and garbage attacks and mammoth shits. It's exhausting, and it's not like *he's* appreciative of it." I glared in the direction of the skinny Great Dane, who was attempting to catch the gold name charm on his collar in his teeth. An impossible feat, given his thick cord of neck muscles. *Stupid dog.* I flushed, embarrassed at the cruel thought. Maybe it was a good thing I wasn't a mother.

His hand tightened on the small of my back, drawing me closer to him, and he kissed me. I softened into the affection, fisting his stiff dress shirt with one hand as my other crept toward the foam carton he'd set down on the smooth wood dresser surface. He let out a soft groan, and our kiss deepened, our mouths colliding with increasing urgency. I bit gently on his lip, then flicked my tongue inside his as I stealthily worked open the styrofoam lid. He slid his hand down the back of my dress pants and gripped my ass as my fingers closed on an egg, a crack already raised under my explorative touch.

I lifted away from his mouth and slapped his face, the egg in my palm, the yolk splattering across his cheek and nose.

"Fuck!" He jerked away from me, and touched his cheek, picking a piece of shell off and examining it for a long moment before his gaze dropped to the open container. I grabbed a second egg before he had a chance to react.

"You like that outfit?" He grabbed for my waist as I fled, lifting me off the floor as if I was a child. "Because I'm about to rip it off of you."

"No!" I screamed, slamming the second egg on top of his head, disturbing the perfect mold of his close-cropped blond tufts as he swept a hand over the piles of paperwork on the table. I heard the cascade of pages right before my back slammed against the polished wood. "This is fucking Ann Taylor. If you—"

The buttons popped off my shirt like the legs of a can-can line, stunning me into silence. He paused, his eyes devouring my exposed stomach and lace bra.

"You have problems, you know that?"

He pulled at one of my high heels, then the other, tossing both in the general direction of the kitchen. One hit his framed Pudge Rodriguez rookie card and cracked the glass. "You should have taken these off. You might have gotten away from me then."

I lifted my chin. "Maybe I didn't want to get away."

His fingers undid the button on my pinstriped slacks with the ease born of a thousand actions. Ignoring the zipper, he gripped the waist and hooked his fingers underneath the hem of my panties. "Lift your hips."

I planted my feet on his chest and obeyed, inhaling as he skimmed the pants and panties down my legs. He lifted my knees and leaned forward, gently caressing my bare mound with his mouth, his breath tickling the delicate skin, his tongue playing along my opening as he spread my knees further. I gasped out his name, my hand stealing into his hair and tugging on the sticky strands. Tilting my pelvis deeper into his mouth, I cursed as his tongue dipped inside of me, his face buried in me.

My husband loved going down on a woman. I certainly wasn't the first. In addition to rumors of his dick, praises of his oral skills had circled the sorority houses with impressive consistency. The last seven years had honed his skills to custom-fit my needs. His mouth could make me come a dozen different ways, as quickly or as slowly as he deemed necessary. He wouldn't let me come now. I knew it, yet still clawed at his shirt, trying to keep his head between my legs, even as he straightened up, a cocky smile crossing those damp lips.

He reached to the side, his fingers digging into the open carton as his eyes held mine. I moved to my elbows and tried to shimmy back. "Easton..."

He crawled onto the table with surprising ease, and I gripped the edge with one hand, concerned about the additional weight. The wood creaked, then held. Moving above me, he tossed the egg into the air, then caught it. "You remember those shakes you used to make for me?"

"The protein shakes?" Every day of his first spring training season, I'd woken up at dawn with him. That was back when I'd abandoned law school to dive into the life of a baseball wife. Head nutritionist was my first role, one I had managed with the precision of a rabid elephant.

"Right. See, you see eggs as an ingredient. Or..." He frowned, glancing down at his shirt. "A weapon." He pressed on my shoulder with his free hand, pinning me back onto the table. "But I see this as a snack." He cracked the egg on the table's edge, then opened it above me, letting the thick yolk drip over my cleavage and stomach.

I tried to squirm away from the cold liquid. "E—"

He lowered his mouth onto my collarbone and sucked along my skin, his tongue swiping and flicking as he moved. He kissed, teased and bit his way along the egg's path, his mouth growing rougher, his body settling atop mine, my arousal heating as he clawed my bra down and centered his attention on my right nipple, then my left. I yanked at his tie, my fingers wet yet efficient as I freed the noose from his neck and undid the top button. Lifting his head off my breast, he reached over his head and tugged at the back of his shirt, yanking it from its tuck and pulling it over his head, his tan and muscular torso suddenly exposed.

His belt and pants were next, the buckle clanking loudly against the wood, our bodies repositioned as I wrapped my legs around his waist and he gripped the top edge of the table and thrust forward, pushing his cock in.

It wasn't smooth. It hurt, my vertebra crunching against the unyielding table. A page that didn't make it to the floor was stuck to my cheek, egg dried on my stomach, and his head slammed into the chandelier at one point, but it was motherfucking hot. Animalistic. Raw. He grunted as he rode me, his dick beyond hard, my body greedy and ready, our mouths finding each other for frantic kisses at odd intervals. I broke first, clawing at his chest as I cursed my way over the peak of orgasm, my heart hammering in my chest as pleasure pulsed through me. He followed a few minutes later, his breath hot in my ear, his body lowering to mine as he gave a few final thrusts.

"Don't move," he ordered, his voice annoyingly level. I was panting like a winded grandma and he was in perfect control, his heart beating at a strong and regular pace, his skin barely damp with sweat. Would I ever be able to budge his endurance needle? Maybe I should be grateful. My sister's husband had wheezed after we'd sprinted from one gate to the other in the Miami airport. She once told me that sex with him involved intermissions, and not because he lasted too long.

Rolling off of me, he maneuvered over a sea of paperwork, stepping from bare spot to bare spot as if he was playing a game of hot lava. He disappeared around the corner and I let my legs splay open, the delicate trickle of air from the overhead vent gloriously cool on my overheated skin.

"We're out of paper towels," he announced, back with a box of Vick's VapoRub Kleenex. I lifted up my head and glared at him. "Don't use a tissue. Just—" I held up one hand as I tried to sit up. My hand hit a slick patch of egg and I slammed onto my back, the impact knocking the breath out of me. I huffed out a pained cry.

"Here." The tissue box tossed aside, Easton trudged through a pile of receipts and worked his hands under me, carefully lifting me into his arms. "I'll carry you to the shower."

I looped my hands around his neck. "And buy me a new shirt," I instructed, trying not to think about the eighty-dollar button-up that he'd just ruined. So much for reducing our credit card charges this month.

"I'll buy you five new shirts," he promised me, and I forced a smile.

"Better thought, I'll pick out a new shirt and send you the bill." I traced his features with my fingers, bringing the laser focus of those blue eyes to me. "I love you."

"I love you too," he said gruffly, his hands tightening on me as he leaned in for a kiss. Sidestepping through the hall, he carried me toward our bedroom, his shoes sticking along the wood floor as he moved. We passed the living room and I heard the faint sound of the television, the talk show host discussing the traditions on Mother's Day.

Mother's Day. It was stupid for me to have wanted a card that badly. I'd wanted to turn the attention off our lack of a baby and onto our Marmaduke of a dog. I had thought that a big stink over a card might distract him from the insufficiencies of my eggs. But that had been stupid. Instead, I'd drawn giant red arrows to my flat stomach, our nursery-turned-office, our high-chair-free dining room.

Maybe it didn't matter. Dr.Phil said that not all men want children. Maybe Easton was happy with things as they were, maybe he liked interruption-free nights, and couples vacations, and the ability to party and fuck, as often and freely as we liked.

Maybe. Maybe. Maybe.

I tightened my grip on him, all the same.

I stood in the shower, water running over my sticky skin, and tried to enjoy the aftershocks of our lovemaking. But something felt off, and I closed my eyes under the spray, trying to pinpoint what it was. We had been as passionate as always, my confidence in our marriage always solidified by our sex. And the fight, of course, had only made it hotter. Our fights always seemed to end with us naked, our anger dissolving as our orgasms mounted.

I rubbed an exfoliating scrub into my cheeks and tried to place what was still nagging at me about this event. Was it the subject matter itself? My insecurities over my fertility issues? His avoidance of the topic altogether? Or... oh. The realization came with startling clarity.

It was the first time, in almost a year, that we'd had sex without me thinking—at least for a brief moment—of someone else.

6

I think you have to properly experience cheating in order to form a valid opinion on it. As either the cheater or the cheatee. It's like death or a cancer diagnosis. Unless you're in the trenches, facing the possibility or actuality, it's not real. It's a concept, one you can judge from afar and gossip over for hours without actually understanding the depth of feelings and emotions that are involved in the event.

I watched my husband as he spoke on the phone, his handsome features pinching, his one-sided dialogue giving me clues to the conversation. Cheating was the topic and with Aaron on the other side of the line, I knew who the culprit was—Becca.

"When's he following her? Today?" Easton's eyes cut to me, and he gave me a pained look.

I picked up my setting and headed to the kitchen, scraping the remnants of the spaghetti into the trash. Wayland looked worriedly from my plate to the trash can, then whined. Setting the rose-dotted china on the floor, I watched as he quickly cleaned every bit of the meat sauce off the delicate saucer, the eBay find scraping against the red Spanish tile as he skidded it into the corner and tried to pin it in place with his paw.

"Let me know what happens. I'm sorry, man. I hate that you have to deal with this."

From behind me, I heard his chair squeak against the tile as he pushed away from the breakfast table and headed toward me. Shooing Wayland away, he picked up the plate and set his own down.

"Okay. Call me then." He ended the call.

"Becca?" I guessed, taking my plate from him and running it under the hot water.

"Yeah. She's being sketchy with a guy at work. Aaron thinks she's having an affair."

I did quick math on their relationship. They were about to celebrate their third wedding anniversary, if I was calculating things correctly. "Cheating already? That's quick."

He rescued his plate from Wayland and passed it to me. "Yeah. I hope he's wrong, but Aaron isn't paranoid. Everything he's describing sounds suspicious."

And Easton wasn't a suspicious guy. Both he and Aaron were, if anything, a little too laissez-faire with their trust. Not that I wanted an overbearing jealous husband, but I sometimes intentionally provoked him, just to get a glimpse of his alpha male side.

Maybe Becca was doing the same thing. Flashing red flags just to get attention. That seemed more likely than a scenario where she would cheat on Aaron. I ran the plate under the hot water. "What's she doing?"

"She's working out constantly. She's started going out with friends and coming home late. She's on her phone all of the time."

I frowned. Becca's friends weren't the type to go out. And anytime Chelsea and I had ever invited her anywhere, she'd always staunchly refused, her social group focused on volunteer opportunities and cooking circles. I tried to picture a new version of Becca, one with a drink in hand, social media popping, without the extra fifteen pounds she'd picked up in college. I couldn't see it.

"Here." Easton came up behind me and kissed the back of my neck. "Let me do these." He reached into the soapy water and stole the sponge from me.

"Okay." I went to move, but he caged me in.

"Stay. I'll work around you." His chest settled against my back and he moved closer to the sink, pinning me in as he looked over my shoulder and into the sink. There were only a few items. The big spaghetti pot. The spoon and spatula. Our plates and silverware. I leaned back into his chest, letting him work and examining our reflection in the plate-glass window above the sink. So handsome, my husband. This lighting was good for me too. It hid my acne scars from high school and the bump in the bridge of my nose. He was always better looking than me, and seemed to be getting even more so with age.

"I just can't believe she'd cheat on him. She was always so..."

"Bitchy?"

I smiled. "So much of a prude. And so superior to everything." Especially deviant behavior. When Aaron had passed out at his bachelor party and had to be carried home, she had flipped out and called us children, then fired Chelsea and me from bridesmaid duty.

"Well, people change. We've changed."

Yeah, we certainly had. In seven years, how had I changed so much? When had I taken on so much stress? So much insecurity? I thought that I would become more secure as I grew older, but I felt as if I was untethered. Careerless. Childless. Useless. I felt, at rare and isolated moments, that I had made a mistake, in everything. And I saw the same fears in my husband. Maybe that's why we held such a strong bond. Both of us continually afraid that we weren't good enough for the other.

"To be honest, I never liked her anyway." He ran the sponge

over the big spoon in a careless motion that would require me to go behind him later.

"I just hate the idea that she'd do that to him."

He didn't respond, and my thoughts flitted back to my earlier hypothesis—that unless you experience cheating, it's too fluid of a concept to really understand. My golden husband had never been cheated on, not by any of his college flings and certainly not by me. Despite my rampant imaginary scenarios, I would never cross that line, not when I knew the emotional pain it delivered. Prior to Jonah cheating on me, I'd been almost cocky. Emotionally indestructible. Fearless in my confidence with relationships and the opposite sex—like Easton still was.

"He's having her followed, so he can see what happens when she goes out tonight." He placed a short quick kiss on the back of my neck.

"Have you ever thought about cheating on me?" The question came out unexpectedly and surprised me as much as him.

He flipped off the faucet and turned me around to face him. "No. What made you ask that?"

"I don't know." I looped my hands around his neck and looked up at him. "Maybe you've had regrets that we got married. Or maybe you're bored."

"No." He slid his wet hands under my shirt, ghosting his fingers over my breasts, bare under one of his baseball tees. "Definitely not bored."

Was I? The internal question hit me as unexpectedly as the one before it, and I pushed it to the side. I wasn't sure it was possible to be bored when constantly trying to keep up with everything.

"What's the closest you ever came to cheating on me?" I moved aside and reached for the bottle of wine that still sat on the counter. Tugging on the cork, I refilled my glass.

He didn't respond, and I plucked another glass from the cabinet and poured the rest of the bottle in it, then pushed it in front of him. "Come on. I'll tell you if you tell me."

That caught his attention, his gaze staying on me as he slowly circled the counter and settled on a stool. Pulling the glass toward him, he picked up the delicate stem and regarded it for a moment before tossing back the golden liquid. "The closest I ever came to cheating on you," he said slowly.

"Yep." I rested my elbows on the counter and leaned forward, meeting his eyes.

"You go first," he said warily.

I wanted to laugh. He should know better than to think this was a trap. I'd never been a conniving sort and blunt honesty had been the bedrock that had built our relationship when I had been too gun-shy to trust another man.

Well, I considered. Blunt, but not *complete* honesty. After all, Easton had no idea of the fantasies I had, the hundreds of men who I'd envisioned above and in me. Some things, my mother once told me, were better off being kept from your husband. That had been her marriage advice, uttered over a spiked ice tea, right before she shot my father a look that was utterly devoid of affection. I'd always assumed my fantasies about other men fell in that 'keep from your husband' category. But maybe this conversation belonged there also.

I tilted back my own glass and took a small sip of the wine. "It was with Jonah," I said finally, setting down the glass. "Senior year. He was in town to move his sister's stuff and came by my apartment."

His eyes sharpened. "You told me that."

"Yeah, but I didn't tell you everything."

His hands tightened on the counter's lip. I watched the muscles in his forearms flex and felt a spike of pleasure shudder through me. "What did you do?"

An interesting way to word it. What did I do? Sexist, really, to put the blame so solidly on me, versus Jonah. Besides, I didn't do anything. It was all Jonah. "I didn't do anything. But he tried to get me too. He wanted to have sex. He kissed me. I pushed him away."

His jaw tightened. "That was it?"

"We talked for a while. Argued. He said I was making a mistake with you. That he still loved me. Stuff like that."

"How close did you come to doing something with him?" His voice had dropped an octave, turning gruff and possessive. He was mad, but struggling to hide it, and my heart swelled at the protective claim in the reaction.

"Close." I ran my finger around the top rim of the glass. "I wanted to. I knew that you'd never find out. And I felt this urge to teach Jonah a lesson. I wanted him to realize what he was missing. I wanted to fuck his brains out and then tear him down. Send him on his way and tell him that I was getting it a lot better with you."

"But you didn't."

"No." I brought my finger to my mouth and sucked on the end of it. His gaze followed the motion. "Your turn."

He didn't want to talk. He wanted to fuck, to reclaim me as his. I could see it in the way he gripped the stool in between his legs with one hand, the other roughly running through his hair. "Ummm..."

"Think carefully." I moved to his side of the counter and hoisted myself on the counter, hanging my legs over the side of it as I sat before him.

"Probably last—" he hesitated, tripping over the word for a moment. "Last year. There was this woman in Idaho. At the FA symposium." His hand found my knee and squeezed the soft fabric of my sweats.

I remembered the symposium. I'd originally planned to go with him, but had come down with something a few days before the weekend. I'd spent the weekend in bed, relieved to be left out of the boring financial conference. "She was an attendee?"

"I don't know. She was at the hotel bar. Saturday night, after you went to bed, I went down there."

Saturday night I'd gotten Panera to deliver a bowl of chicken soup and had popped enough NyQuil to knock me out for twelve beautiful hours. Easton could have fucked an entire cheerleading team in our bedroom and I would have been oblivious to it. I looked down at his hand, still on my knee, and considered pushing it off.

I cleared my throat. "And?"

"And she made it very clear what she wanted."

"Did you flirt with her?"

He hesitated and I saw the truth in the pause, even before he said it. "Yes."

Emotion flooded through me, a complicated mix of jealousy and arousal. It had been too long since I'd been on the receiving end of that flirtation. I could still remember the high it brought, the drag of his eyes across my skin, the look he gave that had burned right through my clothes. I bet she did make her needs clear. I bet she whispered everything she wanted in his ear. Did she run her hand over his crotch? Did her eyes widen as she realized what he was packing in his pants?

I opened my knees wider and used my foot to hook the edge of his stool, tugging it toward me. It didn't budge, but he saw the action and moved it forward.

"What did you say to her?" I pulled at his shirt until he was standing before me.

"Nothing much. I told her she was beautiful."

That hurt, and I yanked at his belt with unnecessary aggression. "Was she?"

"Yes." He watched me get the leather loose from the clasp. "I told her that I was married."

"And?" I flipped the button fly open and tugged on the zipper.

"And she said she didn't care."

He was in my hand then, his breath hissing through his teeth as I wrapped my fist around him.

"I told her I couldn't do anything to her."

"But you wanted to."

"Yes."

"What did you want to do to her?"

His hands settled on my thighs and slid up to my hips, finding the drawstring waist. "I wanted to make her come."

"And?"

He swallowed. "And I wanted her to see my dick."

"You wanted her to see how big it was?" He was growing stiff in my hands. I squeezed it, feeling the rigidity, and watched as his eyes shuttered closed.

"Yes," he gritted out.

"I'm glad you didn't show it to her." I kissed his neck and worked my hand along his shaft.

"I never would."

I fully believed that, fully trusted him. But I didn't blame him for having the desires. He'd had three years at Florida State of showing his cock to dozens of women. He'd heard the gossip that had spread, had been puffed like a peacock by the time he started dating me. But then we'd become exclusive. Gotten married. His dick had become the sole property of me, and I had grown accustomed to the girth and size of it. It wasn't crazy to think that, like me, he craved the unique attention and idolization of a complete stranger.

I couldn't give him that, but I could do the next best thing. I moved down his body and dropped to my knees in the middle of our kitchen. Pulling him toward me, I gave his dick the worship it properly deserved, and pictured Jonah watching us the entire time, his face dark with jealousy, his eyes on Easton's huge cock.

7

At some point, my reluctant ovaries would combust, and I would blame that moment entirely on the woman who created them. Switching my call to Bluetooth, I set the cell phone in the cupholder and stared at the gridlock of traffic before me.

"I'm telling you, you've got to watch your age. Once you hit 31, you might as well pack up the baby strollers and forget it. Your twenties are the golden time! A few more years, honey. That's all you have left." My mother's voice pitched in height, the way it did when she was nagging my father about his driving, and I suddenly understood why he stopped wearing his hearing aids.

"It's not like it used to be, Mom. We don't have to have a baby to be happy." If I didn't think Easton would see it, I'd put a post-it with that phrase on my bathroom mirror, just to constantly remind myself of the fact. *We don't have to have a baby to be happy. We don't have to have a baby to be happy. We don't have to have a baby to be happy.*

Here was another one. *I don't have to have a baby to be valuable.* That pearl of wisdom came, surprisingly enough, from Ling, who was already two babies in, despite all of her wide-eyed innocence in college. I'd written down her advice and hidden it in my desk drawer, right next to my ovulation calendar.

"I know you're having sex, with that orangutan of a husband. And one in four women will get pregnant in any single menstrual cycle, Elle. Just time your sex accordingly. I had sex with your father once in 1991, once. That was all it took!"

No wonder Easton felt insecure around my mother. I took a deep breath and tried not to scream when the car ahead of me turned on its flashers. "I wish you wouldn't say things like that."

"Well, we did. One time. His birthday, of course. As if being born is something that needs to be commended."

"I'm not talking about that. I'm talking about Easton. My husband."

"I don't even know what I said. Can you just listen to me? Can you? I'm not getting any younger here, and neither are you. Lizzie Sommers has two, and her daughter-in-law is *Chinese*."

"I'm really not sure what that has to do with anything."

"Is it a sperm issue? You know, I always suspected that Easton smoked marijuana. It's very common among athletes, according to Margie."

"MOM. Please." Not that we hadn't had our own fears about that issue. Fears that were quickly dissolved by a doctor's test which showed my husband to be an Olympic athlete of sperm production.

"And what's he doing now? I saw on Facebook that he's changed companies again. Did he get fired?"

"It's the same company. They just merged with someone else and changed names." Here it was, the transition of our conversation from my childless state to criticism of my husband. I was tired of it. Tired of all of it. Was there a point in life when you could fire your parents? How long did you have to appreciate their sacrifices for? I made a mental vow, if I ever could conceive and birth a child, to respect their decisions and keep my opinions to myself.

"I just don't think that finance is the right job for him. He's not a numbers person. Remember your wedding? The catering bill? When he didn't calculate in the service fee?"

Oh my God. It'd been five years. And back then, we'd been blowing money as if we were made of it. All things I couldn't tell my mother, not when I was working my ass off to maintain the carefully fabricated illusion that we were still financially secure.

I bit back a response and moved into the turn lane, tailing a yellow Prius with more Bernie Sanders stickers than paint. "Mom, I'm late to a dermatologist appointment and in horrible traffic. Let me focus on the road and I'll talk to you later."

There was the customary disappointed silence, then a big sigh of defeat. "Fine. I'll tell your father that you said hi."

I added on an extra *I love you,* and still left the conversation feeling guilty and insufficient. Maybe that was every mother's duty —to make us better by pointing out our deficiencies. If so, she had nailed motherhood from the start, and I had big plans to skip that duty altogether.

I stood still, my bare feet curling against the cool tile floor, and waited as the doctor ran his hands down my back. "This..." he said thoughtfully. "Have you been keeping an eye on this?" He swirled a finger around a spot on the middle of my back. "I don't remember seeing it at our previous session."

I twisted to look in the full-length mirror, unable to see the item in question. "I'm not sure."

He wheeled back and lifted his clipboard, consulting my last exam sketch. "I'm going to take a photo of it for now." He set down the board and moved closer. There was a quick flash and the sound of a shutter.

I faced forward again, closing my eyes as he moved my hair to one side and ran a rough thumb over the spot. He hummed in contemplation.

"Do you need me to undo my bra?"

I felt both of his hands now, running under the band of my bra and sliding the delicate fabric up by an inch. "No, I can work around it." The new position made the underwire cut into my ribs, and I looked down to see my breasts projected out at an exaggerated angle. I wasn't a busty girl, but at this angle, I looked freakishly stacked.

"Nothing there." He moved the bra strap back into place and sighed as his fingers ran down the curve of my lower back, hitting the top seam of my panties. I'd dressed with this appointment in mind. Black lace had seemed too sexy, so I'd gone with white cotton, the panties a flattering but modest bikini style - the bra a conservative style with a hidden underwire.

I imagined his hand drifting lower, pulling my panties to the side and sliding his touch along the crack of my ass. *Bend forward, Mrs. North. This may require a more thorough exam.* He'd part me with those long talented fingers. Dip one inside me and marvel at the tight fit. Then a second. *Have you always been so responsive, Mrs. North?*

Do you like it when I touch you there?

How about here?

I steeled myself against the fantasy, trying to push it away and focus on a container of cotton balls, set along the back of the counter. I didn't need this, not right now. I pinched my eyes shut and it forced its way back in.

He'd push his fingers in deeper and grow hard, his cock jutting against those loose scrubs, the prick of it bumping against my leg as he moved around me. He'd shift his stance and reach down to adjust it. Glance at the door and struggle with the moral dilemma.

He wouldn't be able to resist. Not when I sat back on the exam table and opened my legs. Not when he saw the damp spot on the crotch of my panties, the evidence of my need. Not when I unclipped my bra, and pulled the straps off my shoulders, and let him see the breasts he kept sneaking semi-professional peeks of.

He'd groan. Hesitate again. His hand would settle on his crotch. He'd tease the shaft through the material. He'd give one final glance at the door. Then he'd tug the drawstring waist of his pants down. He'd step forward. *Lay back*, he'd growl. *I'm going to give you exactly what you want.* I bet he's big. I bet behind those wire-framed glasses and nerdy haircut, there was a beast of a cock, waiting to be unfurled. I bet he's dirty. His grip would probably close around my throat. He'd clamp a hand over my mouth to stifle my cries. He'd lean forward, right as he pushed inside of me, and call me a *dirty little slut*.

I parted my feet slightly as he ran the tip of his pen along my butt cheek, pulling the underwear higher to expose more skin.

"Anything I need to know about here?"

"Not that I know of." I tried to chuckle. "But I also didn't know about the freckle you just took photos of. It's hard to see my butt."

"Have your husband check you every other month or so. In between our appointments. With your family history, it's important that we stay diligent."

We. I thought of him doing the exam with Easton. Easton would scowl at the easy familiarity the doctor had with my body. He'd stop his hands before they got anywhere close to my ass. I'd have both of their attention, both of their eyes, both of their hands, running over me at the same time. I bit my lip to keep my breathing in check, the idea one that was practically making me pant.

"Turn around, Mrs. North." He stayed on the low stool, and when I turned, he was at eye level with my hips.

He played a good game. Dr. Richards was strictly professional. All business. It only made the fantasy hotter, only made me question the boundaries more. I didn't buy the gold wedding band or the ironed scrubs, his geeky Timex with the 24-hour time setting on. Fuck the fancy med school diploma on the wall. He'd chosen a profession where he could put his hands all over women. He liked for us to undress in his office and stand before him, shivering under the too-cool thermostat that he set himself. Tonight, maybe he'd beat off to me. He'd picture me just like this and grow hard. Fist his cock and imagine my mouth, my skin, my wet and tight pussy.

I clenched my inner muscles and couldn't stop the tremor that hit me when his hand landed on my upper thigh. I kept my eyes on the floor, but felt the blush hit my cheeks. Had he noticed?

"You look good, Mrs. North. Everything here is staying similar in size. I don't see any biopsy needs on this visit."

He stood, his eyes critically moving over my cleavage, even though he'd already covered that ground.

"I think you should come back in a month, just for another look at that new spot on your back. Unless you want to just keep me posted, and have your husband check it." His eyes met mine.

"No, I'll come in." I laughed. "My husband doesn't have great attention to detail. It could be the size of a quarter and he wouldn't notice."

He smiled. "Then I'll see you in a month."

He left me to dress and I flipped the lock on the door, lying back on his exam table and shoving my panties down to my thighs. Rubbing my fingers gently over my clit, I gave in to the illicit fantasy. I closed my eyes and thought of his touch. Imagined that he had a camera hidden in the vents. He was probably back in his office right now. Barely able to shut the door before he had his dick out, swollen with need, the tip of it wet with pre-cum. I straightened my legs, my body tensing, and thought of him watching me, his eyes widening at the view. He'd barely make it to his desk chair before his nuts would tighten, his orgasm close. Mine was close. My body was humming, my nipples pricked and sensitive in the cool air, my feet arching as I almost lifted off the examining table and into my hand.

He wouldn't be able to hold back the groan. He'd shoot his release all over his desk, all over important documents and client files and test results. He'd keep coming, his eyes glued on the screen, glued on the image of me, and he wouldn't care, wouldn't think about anything except how badly he wanted me—

My orgasm crested, my touch softening, my back arching as the waves of pleasure bundling and breaking, my body sinking into the padded plastic as they ebbed, then fell away.

My hand fell away from my soaked opening, and I lay there for one long moment, recovering.

Recovering… and hating myself for what I had become. Insatiable and freaky. I had a porn star of a husband and still couldn't keep my imaginary knees together.

Easton didn't know it, but I'd stopped taking my fertility drugs three months ago in an attempt to curb the fantasies. They hadn't stopped. If anything, they were getting stronger. More frequent. More insistent. Prior fertility drugs, I'd been able to have a fleeting attraction and move on without a second thought. Last week, I'd temporarily shut down an open house so I could *finger* myself in the powder room, my head clogged with filthy thoughts of the owner coming back early and catching me.

I had to do something. I couldn't continue like this, not without getting caught by someone.

A cart rattled in the hall and I rolled over with a contented sigh, then got dressed.

8

I hovered my palm over the horn, prepared to lay on it if the Maserati ahead of me got any ideas. "Keep going," I urged under my breath, hissing out a breath as I watched the nose of the purple sports car ease toward the only parallel spot on Lincoln. Its brake lights flared and then went dark, the engine sounding as the driver gunned it forward. I whipped my wheel to the left, then right, ignoring the irritated horn of the car behind me as I maneuvered my snub-nosed coupe into the tight spot. Lifting my hand, I waved my thanks to the impatient driver, then jerked the shift knob into park.

Opening the car door, I was hit with the full force of the Miami humidity. The heat was like a wool blanket, clawing up my skin and working its way under my loose chiffon top. I stuck one wedge-clad foot out, then the other, sticking close to the car as I eased out and avoided the lane of traffic that flew by.

Rounding the back end of the BMW one-series, I hit the lock button on the fob, averting my eyes at the cheap beep it made. It was bad enough on our tree-lined street where old money kept classic Rolls Royces in their four-car garages. At this address I'm a different kind of pathetic—the sort overshadowed by flashy wallets who see my intro Beamer as what it was—an attempt to sit at the big kids table despite my saggy diaper.

"Elle!" Chelsea called out from a table under a striped umbrella. I waved at her and navigated past the hostess stand and through the crowded street-side patio. On Lincoln Ave, space was expensive, and I accidentally whacked at least two people with my bag before I made it to Chelsea.

"No seats inside?" I tossed the bag under the table and sank into the opposite seat. Grabbing the menu, I fanned at my neck.

"Nope. But the misters are on. Just sit there a minute, you'll feel them." She lifted a pale pink concoction to her lips. "I got you a mojito."

"Great." I glanced at my watch. "Sorry I'm late. The home inspector didn't show up until ten and took forever."

"It's fine." Chelsea waved off the ten minutes without concern. "I've been flirting with the waiter. He and I are in total agreement that you are a thoughtless bitch, so be sure to play the role up."

I let out a laugh. "No problem. I'm feeling like a total thoughtless bitch. By the way, you're buying lunch and I want the tuna appetizer."

"There's my bitch." She smiled at me. "And I already ordered the tuna appetizer so find something else to be difficult about."

"Hmm..." I crinkled up my nose. "Give me time. I'll come up with something."

"Mojito?" The drink was delivered by a very dark-skinned man who filled his green golf shirt to perfection. He smiled at me. "Welcome to Papitos."

Chelsea tugged on the man's sleeve, then launched into a detailed quiz about the gluten-free options on the menu. I ordered, then sat back in my chair and took a moment to let out the morning's tension.

This closing would be the death of me. Two weeks over contract on a house that I desperately needed to sell, and my sellers were being cheap. The home inspection had been one long breath-holding procedure where I waited for the inevitable bad news, then got exactly what I'd expected. Aluminum wiring in the attic and polybutylene pipes in the downstairs bath. It would cost ten thousand to repair, if not more. Ten thousand dollars on a contract where I'd already eaten a grand of commission, just to seal the deal.

"Have you ever been with a black guy?" Chelsea popped the question at normal volume, then stuffed a piece of bread in her mouth. Bread that most certainly contained gluten, despite the interrogation she just put the menu through.

I eyed the bread and considered my own avoidance of carbs, one that was on a twelve-day streak. "Uh—no."

"They're gooood," she mused through a mouthful of bread, the word stretched out and savored, her head turning to watch as our waiter eased by and to an adjacent table, a pitcher of ice water in hand. "Very athletic."

I tore the teeniest corner off the top of a roll and dug it through the mound of butter, biting back my opinions on the comment. Chelsea had once had political aspirations—a short-term career she abandoned around the time that the first #metoo accusations started to fly. We had sat her down over margaritas and tacos and explained very gently that she was a walking and talking offense and sexual harassment machine. She'd listened to our points with rapt attention, then ordered a round of tequila shots and toasted to promiscuity and world peace.

"Speaking of good..." she held up a finger and swallowed the piece of bread, then continued. "How is that delicious husband of yours?"

"He's fine." I set down the cold glass. "Please don't compare him to any black men you've screwed. I'd like to pretend, at least until I get something to eat, that you haven't slept with my husband."

It was an ill-timed comment, my airy retort landing square in the face of the elderly man who paused at our table. He hesitated, his gaze darting from me to Chelsea, then smoothed a hand down his tie and began to speak.

"Miss Pedicant?"

Chelsea straightened up in her seat. "Mr. Bronson. How wonderful to see you. Are you with your wife?"

"Sadly, no." He gave me a polite smile and I half rose in my seat, offering my hand and introducing myself. Turning his attention back to Chelsea, he started to ease past. "Please tell your father that I said hello. We have big plans for next year and will need his station's full support."

"I'll certainly tell him. Please give my best to your wife."

He nodded at Chelsea, then me, then continued his slow and methodical journey out of the restaurant.

Chelsea waited until he was out of earshot, then spoke. "If you ever want to leave Easton for a billionaire, that's your man right there. Frank Bronson. His wife's our age and has breasts as big as your head."

"Really?" I craned my head to get a final look at the older gentleman. "He didn't seem like that type."

She let out a snort as she reached into her bag. "*Every* man is that type, it's just a question of if they have the money and the balls to pull it off." She pulled out her phone. "Let me text my dad real quick. He's going to want to know that I saw him."

"It wasn't exactly the best moment for him to enter our conversation," I said dryly.

She smiled as her fingers darted over the screen. "I know, right? Did you see his face?"

The absence of concern was one of the reasons I loved her. It was also, in my stressful moments, one of the more annoying aspects of our friendship. Everything in Chelsea's life seemed to be fixed by money or sex. She worked for her father's media conglomerate and enjoyed unchallenged job security, her own hours, a never-ending bank account, and enough one-night stands to impress even the most voracious sluts.

The tuna appetizer was delivered and I pulled my chair closer to the table, eagerly diving into the tartare mountain.

"Before I forget." Chelsea looked up from her phone. "I've got a client for E."

"An athlete?"

"Yep. Nicole Fagnani—heard of her?"

I hadn't, but that didn't mean anything. When it came to professional athletes and sports, my Rolodex of knowledge was pretty slim. "What sport does she play?"

Chelsea gave me an exasperated look. "Tennis, Elle. I swear to God, do you pay any attention to anything? Nicole is the one who tied Agassi in that charity match back in December. *Agassi*, Elle."

I'd heard of Agassi. I struggled to remember why. "He's married to someone famous, right?"

"Oh my God, stop it." She dipped a crisp cracker into the tuna. "Anyway, Nike just signed her to some ridiculous contract and she's doing ad shoots next week. I thought you could come with E, and I could make the introduction."

"Who is her current FA?" I turned over the idea in my head. After Easton was dropped by the Marlin's, he decided to use his finance degree to stay in Miami and advise professional athletes. At least, that was the plan. I swear to God, his entire career plan was hatched after three beers and a single episode of Ballers. Only, unlike Dwayne Johnson and his big house and bevy of exotic cars, we were staring at mounting credit card debt and a house that seemed to be on the verge of collapse.

"Who knows or cares? She'll take one look at your husband and sign up for whatever shit he's peddling." She waved off the concern as if Easton's looks were some magic potion that turned intelligent women into idiots.

Though... I glanced down at the diamond on my left ring finger. I was a pretty shining example of exactly that. When he proposed, he'd been puffed up on dreams of the big leagues. Jets. Packed stadiums. Vacation mansions and household staffs. Ferraris and monster contracts. All things he thought would impress me, but I'd bought into Easton North for an entirely different set of factors—factors he still possessed in spades. Charm. Looks. Wit. Heat. A lethal combination that would be difficult for any woman to resist.

"Is she pretty?"

Chelsea shot me a bewildered look. "Would it matter? Don't tell me you're suddenly insecure about your marriage. You know E's crazy about you. And I thought he needed more clients."

"He does," I said sharply. My husband's client list was scrawny —a few baseball players he'd picked up using every pro connection he had, plus a young golfer who seemed more intent on partying than winning. He'd had a few nice paychecks, but nothing that was easing the tight grip that settled on my chest with each round of monthly bills. "Send him the shoot details. I'll give him a heads up."

"And no," she remarked mildly. "She isn't that pretty. But really, Elle." She cocked a blonde brow at me. "Jealousy is not your color."

Was it anyones? Maybe it was our frank conversation where Easton had told me about his symposium flirt, or my guilt over my rampant fantasies, but I was feeling extra possessive over my husband. And maybe a little insecure, especially where a successful and athletic potential client was involved.

My phone chimed, saving me from a witty retort I didn't have. I made a big show over picking up my bag and shuffling through its contents, moving aside the doomed inspection report and finding the slim phone. "Speak of the devil." I smiled and opened the text from E. Reading the short message, my mood sank.

Just got a call from Aaron. Becca just served him with divorce papers. Says she's in love with someone else.

"Oh my God."

"What?" Chelsea grabbed for my phone, wanting to read the message.

I held it out of her reach. "Becca's divorcing Aaron. She's been cheating on him."

Her eyes widened, exposing her brilliantly applied purple shadow. "And she's leaving him? Why the fuck would she cheat on *Aaron?*"

I thought of yesterday's dermatology appointment. The male barista at the coffee shop I swung by three mornings a week. The fantasies that were starting to batter against my morality every single day. Would I be Becca one day? While I would never leave Easton, would two of my friends incredulously critique my cheating over an appetizer and watered-down drinks?

I unstuck the back of one leg from the plastic seat and crossed my legs, pinning my hands underneath my thighs. "Maybe we should call her."

Chelsea hummed out a bar of trepidation. "I don't know. Aaron's E's best friend. Our alliances seem pretty clear."

Yes, in the world of divisions, the choice was easy. The skanky wife or the grieving husband. Our friend or his cheating wife. What good would an olive branch be? Did she even deserve a friendly gesture?

No, but my heart still broke at the thought of a marriage dying. I looked down at the crisp white tablecloth and deleted the desire to reach out.

"Now," Chelsea announced with the graveness that could only precede a ridiculous statement. "Is it too soon to finally confess my wet dreams about Aaron? Because *oh my God* that boy is delicious."

I barked out a laugh. "Finally confess? You told Becca you wanted him to stuff you like a Build-a-Bear."

"That was a compliment, Elle." She tried to roll her eyes, but ended up laughing instead. "I was trying to break the ice! She was so stiff that night we met her." She straightened in her seat and adopted a southern drawl that no one had used in a hundred years.

"A pleasure to meet you, Chelsea. Though I must say, you *are* wearing white after Labor Day."

"She didn't say that," I protested.

"She wanted to say it. I could *feel* her wanting to say it." She played with the end of her straw. "So I gave her a compliment on her boyfriend." She shrugged. "I wouldn't have done it if they were already married."

"Oh right." I nodded. "That's where you draw the line. Because you've certainly snapped your trap about Easton ever since I walked down the aisle."

"Easton's different," she whined. "I had him first so I'm allowed to gush over his sexual prowess. Plus, I need to remind you of the HUGE sacrifice I made for the sake of our friendship." She held her hands about a foot apart to make the pun perfectly clear. I threw the wrapper of my straw at her.

"Speaking of sacrifice..." she perked up at the sight of our waiter returning, a pitcher of water in hand. "I plan to lay myself bare at our waiter's alter tonight. Be a dear and run to the bathroom, will you? I'm about to—"

"Say no more," I interrupted, pushing to my feet. You only watch Chelsea hit on a man once, and you learn your lesson. I'd had bikini waxes that are less uncomfortable. I grabbed my bag and escaped just in time.

9

Vegas?

Three days later, the one-word text from Chelsea popped up. I yanked at the mailbox door, getting the rusted hinge open. There was a small soft package, tucked among the bills and I stuffed it into my bag and glanced toward the house. Easton wasn't in sight, but his Jeep was in the drive, along with Aaron's crew cab truck, Talbot's Construction printed in red on the side.

I worked the mailbox door shut and unlocked my phone, typing out a quick response.

No.

I didn't know what she's thinking, but our current finances made Vegas a terrible idea right now. Especially with Easton's love of craps.

Dots immediately popped up, followed by an emoji with steam coming out of irritated nostrils. I laughed, then responded.

where r u?

— Leaving High Pines. Got stuck at dads but be there soon.

I sent a thumbs up, then headed toward the house, flipping through the mail as I made my way up our painted concrete drive. I glanced in Aaron's truck as I passed, curious if he had brought a bag. Other than a Big Gulp cup and an overstuffed clipboard, the front seat was empty.

Swinging open our front door, I paused, bracing for Wayland's enthusiastic greeting and Easton's shout. Neither came, and I glanced through the open entryway. "Hello?"

Silence. I kicked back my left foot and pulled off the heel, then did the same with the right. Opening the entry closet, I placed the electric blue pumps on an open spot on a middle shelf, between a gold set of Tieks and some wedge sandals. Reaching into my bag, I pulled out the small package and put it on the highest shelf, pushing it behind a pair of `gladiator sandals I hadn't worn since Selena and Justin first broke up. The package bumped against the one from last month, and I cursed myself for letting another month pass without canceling the fertility drug's autofill. The pills were ridiculously expensive.

Pulling at my shirt, I got it loose from the waist-crunching pencil skirt as I made my way through the dim formal living room. Originally, we'd had plans to knock down these walls and create an open floor plan, one that would look out to the backyard and pool. Maybe it'd still happen one day. For now, we had six rooms that divvied up our living square footage into a choppy plan that would be a bitch to sell. I don't know what people were thinking in the seventies. Maybe they liked to be separated all of the time. Maybe the wife wanted to cook in a square box where she couldn't see anyone, and liked her knees to bump into the tub when she sat down to pee.

Stepping into the kitchen, I spied Easton and Aaron clustered together on the back porch, their heads tilted down, looking at something by their feet. And just like that, the unexpected and unwelcome visual pushed itself forward.

My knees, scraping against the rough stubble of the concrete as I knelt in between them.

Aaron's hand, settling on the back of my head and pulling me in.

The worn fabric of Easton's jeans under my hand, his pose shifting impatiently as I let Aaron guide my mouth onto his rigid cock.

"Take it all," Easton ordered, his voice gruff.

"Jesus," Aaron swore. "Your wife knows how to suck a cock."

I turned away from the window sharply, trying to blot out the visual from my head. Blinking rapidly, I made my way to the slider and pulled it open, pasting a smile across my face. "Hey guys."

They looked over, and a slow smile spread across E's face. "Hey baby."

In between their legs sat Wayland, his chin up, mouth open, his tongue lolling to one side. He saw me and barked, his tail thudding, but didn't move.

"E was telling me about his day," Aaron explained.

"Wayland's day? Or E's?" I navigated around the patio furniture and gave Easton a kiss, planted another one on Wayland's snout, and then hugged Aaron. He was as tall as E, and I had to get on my tiptoes in order to wrap my hands around his neck. "Sorry to hear about everything," I whispered in his ear. He squeezed me tighter in response.

"Thanks." We broke apart. "And Wayland's day."

I glanced at Easton. "Oh no. What did he do?"

"Wayland," he said solemnly, "was kicked out of playtime."

"Kicked out of playtime?" I frowned, crossing my arms and looking down at the dog, who offered me one gigantic paw, his grin pinching shut as he took in my stern expression. As I watched, a long line of drool dripped to the floor.

"He was humping the other dogs," Easton explained. "Mercilessly."

"Oh God." I reached in between the two men and grabbed the roll of paper towels, tearing off a piece and crouching before the Great Dane. I wiped up the drool spot before dabbing the dog's cheek. He tried to eat the paper towel and I thwarted the attempt, wrapping my arms around his chest and giving him a hug. Tugging on his ears, I stood. "Where do you think he learned that?"

"Merciless humping?" Easton cocked one brow and lifted his hands in innocence. "I have no idea."

"Uh-huh." I grabbed his shirt and pulled on it, bringing his mouth to mine. "I'm going to go change."

"Do you mind grabbing me one of E's T-shirts" Aaron asked. "I'm dying to get out of this outfit." He cranked his head to the side and worked open his tie.

I started, suddenly aware of his crisp white shirt and dark navy tie. I hadn't seen him in a tie since our wedding. "Look at you. All fancy." Like Easton, he could rock a tie with the best of them. He had a bigger build than my husband, but it was a nice contrast, the dress shirt tight on his shoulders and biceps. It had been so long since I'd seen him in anything other than a T-shirt and jeans, it took a moment to adjust to the shift. I'd like to say that my fantasies kept their proper distance from my husband's best friend, but I had a construction worker fantasy I'd always earmarked for Aaron. Now, my brain reshuffled its Rolodex, slipping this image into the hot executive file as well.

"Had a meeting at the bank." He grimaced. "Looking at a business loan to buy out Becca."

I sobered at the realization that she owned half of his construction business. "I'm sorry, Aaron. That sucks." I pushed Wayland away before he climbed up my leg. "Have you talked to an attorney yet?"

"I'm not contesting it. We're meeting with a mediator tomorrow to discuss the house and the business. If we can agree on those things, everything could be done in thirty days."

Thirty days, and their marriage would be over. Alarming, how quickly a union could fall apart. I turned away before I started getting emotional at the thought. "I'm going to change. I'll grab you a shirt."

I pulled at the slider and left them alone on the porch.

"Fuck her and her feelings."

I paused behind the pair and tapped the edge of Easton's shoulder with a cold beer. "Here." He turned and I handed over another for Aaron, along with a worn T-shirt of E's that had Florida State Baseball on its front. "Change in the pool bath and bring me your shirt," I instructed, hoping he would follow the order and not strip down right here.

"Yes ma'am." He grinned and took the items. "Thanks."

"Whose feelings are we fucking?"

"Becca's," Easton answered, peeking under the lid of the grill. "I'm trying to convince him to start dating."

"Already?" I perched on the edge of the patio table. "That's too quick."

"He hasn't had sex in three months." Easton raised his eyebrows at me.

"What?" I paused, my own beer just before my lips. "You and Becca haven't had sex in three months?"

He ignored the question and shot Easton a sharp look. "I'm going to go change." He finished off his original beer and tossed it into the trashcan. "Feel free to discuss the patheticness of my life while I'm gone." He ambled in the direction of the outdated half-bath by the pool equipment. It would be cramped quarters, hot as fuck, and crawling with spiders, but I didn't want to risk triggering another fantasy with the sight of his six-pack abs.

"Three months?" I whispered. "Ouch." *No wonder Becca cheated.* As soon as I thought the words, I hated them. Becca had probably been bouncing on her coworker's dick for the past six months, and ignoring Aaron's needs in the process. Another guy might have strayed from the relationship before now, but I knew Aaron's loyalty. He was like Wayland with a toy. Once he made a commitment, he'd ignore everything else, no matter how worn out or dirty or—in Aaron's case—bitchy and sexless—it became.

"You wouldn't last three months," Easton said with a cocky

smile, as if he was the sole source of my sex drive's overanxious heartbeat.

"Neither would you," I shot back.

"He's staying at his mom's house." Easton glanced toward the bath. "She's in New York this week, so it's worked out okay, but next week—" He paused as Aaron came around the edge of the house, his dress shirt in hand, hair mused, Easton's T-shirt a little too tight.

"Are you finished ridiculing me or should I take longer?"

"All done." I took his dress shirt and moved toward the house.

"Let's find you a woman," E said, as if we were replacement parts on a conveyer belt. "I got the perfect girl. Super athletic. Loaded. Single."

I paused just before the back door, curious to see who he was referring to.

"She's that client I'm working on. Nicole Fagnani. The tennis star."

Aaron mumbled something I couldn't catch.

"I'm just starting with her. She's tall, man. You guys would have Amazons as kids."

Nicole Fagnani? I glanced at Aaron, trying to look at him through unbiased eyes, but confirmed what I already knew. He was hot. Really hot. Take a Southern gentleman and put him through ten hours of manual labor each day and you had Aaron—just refined enough to hold open your door but rough and strong enough to fuck you against it.

I'd Googled the tennis star out of pure insecurity, wanting to know who my husband was going to be working with, and let out a relieved breath when the thousands of search results had produced an ordinary looking woman. Mildly pretty, but nothing I needed to lose sleep over.

Aaron pulled out his phone, assumedly to do his own search of the woman. I lingered in the shade of the patio, busying myself with picking dead blooms off my daisy plant.

"She's okay." His words were muffled behind a beer and I took a subtle step closer. "Not Becca."

"It's not her looks," my husband said. "She's just one of those women who have something about them, you know?"

My right shin collided with the edge of the pressure washer and I bit back a yelp of pain, one hidden by the clatter of the spray wand as it hit the floor. They both turned to look at me.

"You okay?" Easton squinted at me.

"Oh yeah," I said breezily, attempting to step forward without hobbling. "I was just cleaning up out here. Thought we could eat outside."

"In this heat?" He waved his beer toward the house. "We can eat in the kitchen."

"Oh." I lifted my shoulder as if I didn't care either way, as if my shirt wasn't sticking to my back from the ridiculous temperatures outside. "Whatever." I moved to the cooler and lifted the lid, grabbing out a bottle of beer and twisting off the lid. "So, she has something about her?"

My husband looked at me as if he had absolutely no idea what I was talking about.

"The tennis player," Aaron prodded.

"Oh. Yeah." Easton turned back to him. "Like a sexual chemistry. Just meet her. You'll see what I mean."

"A sexual chemistry," I repeated, glaring at him.

He laughed. "Not with me. Just in general."

"Uh-huh." My comfort level with his new client suddenly took a sharp right turn.

"To be honest, I can't even think about meeting someone else right now." Aaron opened the grill and peered at the steaks. "I think—"

"Wait." I pointed to Aaron and turned back to Easton. "Is this client going to be a problem?"

"Babe." He set down his beer and placed both hands on my

shoulders, looking into my eyes. "No woman is ever going to be a problem."

"Don't flirt with her," I instructed.

"You told me to flirt with her," he reminded me, and it was an excellent and annoying point. I cringed at the memory of me shoving him out the door with instructions to *close the deal. Flirt with her if you have to.* "That was before."

"Before what?"

"Before I found out that she has some sort of potent sexual chemistry that you feel the need to scamper off and tell Aaron about!" I snapped. "He's right, you know. She's *okay*. Barely pretty." I could hear the insecure cruelty in my words, but didn't care, not in the alarming awareness that my husband found his new client attractive.

"Scamper off?" Easton cocked a brow at me. "I don't scamper. Confidently stride."

"Stroll," Aaron suggested.

"Pace."

"March."

"I like that one." E pointed at Aaron. "March. Very authoritative and decisive."

They're lucky I didn't have that beer still in my hand. I would have dumped it over their heads. I let out a highly controlled exhale and watched Easton's smirk soften. He leaned forward and pressed a gentle kiss on me. I twisted away. "You have nothing to worry about," he said quietly. "You're everything to me."

I knew it, believed it, but still felt a knot of stress unfurl at the words. Feigning irritation, I pushed away from him. "I'm going to get the corn ready. Don't burn the steaks."

"Yes, ma'am," Aaron called out. I glared at him in response, then bit back a smile when he laughed.

10

I decided somewhere around the middle of my ribeye that I hated Becca. Vehemently hated her. The cheating was one thing, and unforgivable in itself. But it was her attitude about it that was sending my fury into a new direction. She was being dismissive to Aaron, as if she didn't have to explain herself to him, as if the last three years of their marriage didn't grant him the right to ask questions about her reasons for filing for divorce. *In love with another man?* THAT WASN'T GOOD ENOUGH.

"So you don't know anything?" I stabbed at a piece of meat. "Nothing about what she plans to do? If she's marrying him? How long they've been seeing each other?"

"She said I need to respect her privacy." He sighed and leaned back in his chair. "Whatever that means."

"But she's not even considering the idea of working through this and staying together?" Chelsea hunched forward, cupping her wine glass with both hands as if it were a cup of coffee.

"I don't know. I tried to talk to her about it and she said I was pressuring her."

I met Chelsea's gaze across the table and could see her mutual contempt. "Honestly, I think we're focused on the wrong thing," I announced, setting down my fork. "Screw begging her to give your marriage another try. Do you even want to stay married to her after this?" My voice rose with each statement, and I watched Wayland tuck his tail between his legs and run out of the room in anticipation of a fight.

"Elle's right." Chelsea popped a crispy chunk of potato into her mouth. "You should be leaving *her*. For two reasons." She stuck out the index finger of her right hand. "One, because she isn't trying to win you back. And two"—her middle finger joined the party—"She wasn't that great of a wife to begin. And falling in love with someone else? Total chicken shit move."

Aaron winced, and I glared at her complete lack of tact.

"We aren't *sure* that she's in love with this other guy." I nudged her leg with my toe in an attempt to punctuate my point. "She could be emotionally confused. Or maybe this is just a mid-life crisis." In her twenties.

"Uh-uh. She's committed to this guy. Or at the least— committed to the idea of abandoning her marriage. If there was a chance Becca wanted to stay married, she'd act completely different." She nodded her way through the rest of her bite, then reached for her wine glass. "The bottom line is, there's only one way to fix Aaron's woes."

The group fell silent as she took a long and dramatic sip of wine, then smacked her lips together. I ignored her theatrics, fairly certain where they were leading.

"Vegas," she announced, a bit of sparkle to the vowels.

"Vegas?" Aaron repeatedly warily.

Easton nodded in enthusiasm, and I wanted to chuck our latest credit card statement at his head.

"This weekend." Chelsea stood for full effect. "We can take my dad's jet. Split a suite. Get Aaron's dick sucked and fucked by every slut on the strip. By the time we bring him home, his heartache will be healed and he won't remember that bitch's middle name." She lifted her wine in a toast. "Come on. Who's with me?"

11

"Has it occurred to anyone that I'm the only one on this plane that could get married this weekend?" Chelsea stood in the middle of the jet and adjusted her crisp white veil.

"I'd marry you," Easton drawled from his spot in one of the leather recliners. "Assuming they allow multiple wives in Nevada."

"And assuming you divorce me and find another wife who is okay with two wives," I shot back playfully.

"I appreciate the proposal, but I could never be a second wife," Chelsea said airily. "I plan on keeping my husband *very* busy." She turned and ran a hand down the small of her back, adjusting the delicate row of roses that hid the zipper. "But I'm serious. Until Aaron's divorce becomes final, I'm the sole hope for a shotgun Vegas wedding."

"I'm no expert," Aaron remarked. "But I feel like the wedding dress might ward off any would-be suitors."

"Good thing I'm not looking for a proposal then." She lifted up the hem of her dress and carefully moved over to the couch, positioning the dozens of layers of tulle into place before carefully sitting down. "I'm going for the bad boys who want to defile an innocent bride."

"I wish I could tell you it was a stupid plan, but watching you attempt it is worth this entire trip." I smiled at her as I tore open a bag of peanut M&Ms. "Anyone want to place bets on her success rate?"

"Wait." She held up her hand before the men could speak. "What determines success? Because I only plan on letting one man inside these virginal thighs this weekend."

"One guy seems too easy," Aaron remarked. "Especially for her."

Chelsea beamed at him. "I'll take that as a compliment."

He lifted his drink to her in response. Ages ago, back when we were in college and attended Easton and Aaron's baseball games—I entertained notions of a Chelsea and Aaron sandwich. Despite her proclamations of attraction, she never moved down that road, and they had settled early on into a sort of brother/sister relationship that contained plenty of teasing, but no sexual chemistry.

I took the place next to her on the couch and offered her the bag of chocolates. "What about five kisses? She has to get five strangers to kiss her."

"Not just kissing. They have to make out with her," Easton amended. "With tongue and groping."

"Oooh…" Chelsea bounced a little in place. "This is going to be fun. Aaron, are you sure you don't want to hone in on this? We can rent you a tux and cast you as a nervous groom."

He waved off the request. "I'm good with watching the spectacle you create. A hundred bucks says you make it to six kisses."

"I'll take that bet," I said, stealing back the M&Ms from Chelsea. "Here." I passed a napkin just in time to stop her from wiping chocolate on her dress. "Where did you get that thing?" It was ridiculous. Pure Cinderella style, with a ribbon belt, enough beading to hide her curves, and so much tulle she couldn't fit into the plane's bathroom stall. She'd made it worse with bright blue eye shadow, pale pink lips, and a tiara.

"It was my aunt's, the one who passed away. I purchased it from the estate to wear to Halloween last year, but then I decided to be—"

"The slutty dinosaur," I finished, because that was a visual I still couldn't get out of my head.

"I was a *dragon*," she retorted. "One of Daenerys's. Anyway"— she gave me a pointed look to let her finish her story—"this ended up being a better use for it anyway."

Oh yes. A much better use than an actual wedding, which I'm pretty sure had never crossed her mind. I pulled back the hem of the dress and looked at her bare feet, the toes painted a neon yellow polish. "What are you doing for shoes?"

12

We were eight hours into Vegas and had only spent forty-five bucks, so I grudgingly agreed to the thirty-foot-long limo that Chelsea *insisted* we needed. Our second option was finding minivan taxis, which she refused to do, especially since this was her wedding weekend and all. Insert eye roll.

It had been a fairly good initial idea. Initial idea. Chelsea decided, after four drinks and a dismal showing at slots, to open up all the extra room to pedestrians who seemed tired of walking. Which was why Easton and I were crammed in the front end of the seat, in between a Chinese family of four, two prostitutes, a drunk Colorado State student who had lost one of his shoes, and a club promoter who'd already given us each four brochures. Chelsea, in the tally of kisses from strangers, was one down, with 28 hours to go. Her current focus wasn't on kissing. She'd latched on to the prostitutes with full intensity and was drilling them about their hours, methods of payment, and what exactly 'fetish-play' involved. The Chinese mother to my right covered her youngest child's ears.

"This is fun, right?" Easton kissed my cheek, his hand curling around my knee. I turned my head toward him and managed an awkward kiss on the lips.

"It is." I smiled. "But I'm worried Aaron isn't having a good time."

We both looked at him, his tall frame stuffed against the door frame, the fingers of his right hand playing with the buttons. One of the prostitutes was beside him, her hand sliding up and down his thigh as she cooed in his ear. He looked miserable. I glanced at Easton. "See what I mean?"

"He never did go for the slutty ones," he whispered. "Look at Becca."

It was true, and maybe that's why he and Chelsea had fallen so naturally into the friend zone. Becca had been all prim and proper, the sort who never missed a Sunday service, or a top button on her cardigan, or an opportunity to stay at home and read rather than go out with friends. Not that I had any issue with a good book, I just didn't clutch my pearls and skip over any of the 'filthy' sections while reading it.

"So then… why are we taking him to a strip club?" The destination, which had sounded logical after three hours of slots and free drinks, suddenly seemed pointless.

"Relax." His fingers played along my bare thigh, pushing the edge of my gold skirt up. "He'll have a good time."

The limo slowed and I tucked my feet in, staying out of the way as the Chinese family crawled out, followed by the two prostitutes. Aaron pulled the door closed and stretched out his legs, glancing from the club promoter to the college kid to us. "Well, this is fun."

"Have we passed Saffire? Hey!" Chelsea crawled toward the front of the limo, giving everyone a faceful of wedding dress along the way, and knocked on the driver's privacy door.

"Is she really getting married?" The college kid asked, staring at Chelsea's butt, which bobbed in the air as she gave our driver a barrage of instructions.

"Yes," I answered, at the same time as Easton and Aaron said "no." I glared at them both in turn, then faced the confused kid. "Yes," I repeated solemnly.

"We're almost there," Chelsea crawled back, her sequined studded heels almost puncturing my left big toe. "And I've got a bra full of cash, so first dance for everyone is on me." She frowned at the two strangers. "Where are we dropping you guys off again? I need to make out with one of you before you leave."

"That didn't count," I argued, sipping on a sour apple martini as I watched Aaron and Easton at the ledge by the main stage. "You can't order someone to make out with you and count it toward your total."

"But he *liked* it," she countered. "And look, I got a drink coupon out of it." She produced a bright orange card out of her bra, then fished out two more. "Technically three drink coupons."

I examined the coupons, which were for a sushi restaurant, and good between four and five pm on Tuesdays. "You do make a compelling argument," I tapped the front of the first card as if in deep thought. "Oh wait, they're expired." I pinned my finger to the handwritten date, which passed last week.

"What?" she squawked, snatching the cards from me and examining the other two. "That's bullshit."

I watched as two strippers sidled up to Easton and Aaron. "We got hunters approaching prey."

"Ooh, let me see." She crawled on top of her stool, and leaned forward as if she were courtside at a Heat game. "They're sexy."

"Yeah." I distracted myself with a long pull of my drink. "If you like big boobs and pretty faces."

"Which of course they don't," she said cheerfully.

Easton turned over his shoulder and glanced at me, raising one eyebrow in permission. I waved him on.

"I read a study once on the psychology of strip club clients,"

Chelsea announced, her useless drink coupons forgotten. "It said that strip club regulars are social masochists. They enjoy the brief high of a certain stripper's affections, but are left unsatisfied, over and over again—that's the pain part."

"Yeah, I got it." I watched as the shorter of the two girls led my husband to a chair and shoved him down into it. He smiled and the jealous piece inside my heart came to life.

"And it's the addictive cycle that begins," she babbled on. "Where they are afraid to stop paying the stripper, because that ends the chance of an emotional or physical consummation." She elbowed me. "Are you listening? Selling the belief that something will happen is what turns the wheel."

I watched as she settled onto his lap, her legs on either side of his, her hips swiveling as she teased him with her sparkly pink crotch. He wouldn't get hard. I knew it, was confident of it, yet my stomach still tightened, my skin growing flush as I pressed closer to the balcony rail that separated our part of the club from their's.

"Excuse me, ladies. Are these seats taken?" The voice was deep and rich, and I glanced over to see two Chippendale-style dancers hovering by our table.

I spoke before Chelsea could open her thighs and invite the both of them to move in. "Yes, our boyfriends are in the bathroom." I gave a regretful smile and reached out, gripping Chelsea's arm to keep her quiet.

She, of course, ignored the gesture. "It's actually my fiancé," she beamed. "Wedding is at midnight tonight." She held out her hand so that the two men in tearaway shorts could examine her ring. I shot my own glimpse at the small diamond boulder and hoped it wasn't real.

After the men had gone, she turned back to me. "Seriously? Sending away perfectly good dick? Do you have no love for me at all?"

I turned back to the lower landing and watched as my husband's hands tightened on the arms of his chair, his face turned up to the stripper as her bare breasts hung heavy in his face. "I didn't want you to be a masochist," I said loudly, over the pounding chorus of a song.

"Look." She touched my arm. "Told you he needed this."

I followed her index finger and spotted Aaron, reclined back in a chair, his hands cupping the breasts of the woman before him. She whispered something in his ear and his eyes met mine.

I gave him a small smile, but he didn't respond. I watched as her hand brushed over his crotch, then gripped him. I looked away.

"Come on," Chelsea tugged at my arm. "Let's go down and show up these bitches."

We were six minutes from Taco Bell when Chelsea realized she didn't have her wallet. I looked up from my phone's GPS program with an alarmed look. "You brought your wallet?" She'd been shelling out twenties from her bra like a broken ATM machine, but I hadn't seen her wallet all night.

"Not the entire thing," she huffed, frantically rapping on the driver's glass. "I clipped the coin purse thingy to my bra. I must have left it in the bathroom stall when I went to pee."

I did have a fuzzy recollection of her fishing her black American Express and driver's license out at the bouncer line. At least, with us flying private, she wouldn't need a driver's license to get home. But still, the thought of finishing this trip without her having that card? She'd be John Wayne without a horse. Thor without his hammer. Carrot Top without his props. I glanced at my watch. "How long ago did you go to the bathroom?"

She pressed her hands against her forehead. "I don't know. Maybe thirty minutes ago. Oh my god. Some stripper has it. I know she does. And the problem is, they could use my ID. I look just like half of them."

I stifled a smile. God love her, but Chelsea was a good eight sizes bigger than any stripper in that place. If any of those girls did try to use her ID, they'd have to talk fast to explain the dramatic weight loss.

"Come on..." she drummed her hands on her knees, looking out the limo's window.

"You want me to call Amex?" I offered. "I could pretend to be you." I knew her social security number and birthdate as well as my own, the result of eight years of best friendship.

"Not yet." The car slowed and she scooted toward the door. "Let me run in and see if it's still in the stall first."

"I can come in with—"

"Stay!" She barked, opening the door and hustling toward the red-carpeted entrance, her wedding gown hitched up above her knees.

Easton closed the door behind her.

Silence fell, then an awkward laugh came from Aaron. "I'll say this," he said, rubbing a hand over his face. "Things are never boring with her." His voice was mellowed from the alcohol, one of his legs kicked up on the seat, his body reclined against the leather seat.

"No." I smiled in agreement. "They aren't."

"It's gonna suck if she doesn't find it." He closed his eyes, resting his head back against the headrest. He'd enjoyed five lap dances on our tab. I'd cut Easton off after his first, straddling the place vacated by the blonde and claiming him as my own. I'd been mildly turned on by watching her dance over him, but been more aroused by the greedy way he'd welcomed me onto his lap, his interest—and dick—awakening the minute I'd run my hands down his chest.

"Are we counting her make-out session with the stripper toward her kiss total?" Easton asked, his hands working along my calf and kneading the muscle there. "You know she'll want to."

"I think we should," I said graciously, feeling bad for her expired coupon-weilding kiss from earlier.

"How has she gotten more tongue than me?" Aaron wondered aloud, his eyes still closed. "That's some bullshit. I was lulled here with promises of..." he waved his hand in the air to encompass Chelsea's crude proclamation.

I tried to remember what she'd toasted to in our dining room. Something about sucking and fucking. I reached over and patted his knee. "Don't worry. The night is still young."

"Too bad I'm old." He winced. "If I wasn't so hungry, I'd be crawling into bed right now."

"I don't like her going in there alone." Easton squeezed my calf, then moved my leg off his lap and to the floor. "I'm going to go and check on her."

I glanced toward the club. "Okay. Call me if anything happens."

"Will do." He gave me a quick kiss and opened the door. "Lock this behind me."

"I'll protect her," Aaron called out, lifting a feeble hand in acknowledgment.

Easton chuckled in response and met my eyes just before he shut the door. *Lock it*, he mouthed.

I nodded, hitting the button as soon as he shut the door. Moving back to my spot, I gently nudged Aaron's leg, stirring him to life. "You okay?"

He gave me a slow smile. "After that many drinks?" He snorted. "I'm good. Numb but good."

"You're allowed to grieve," I said quietly. "I know how much you love her." I didn't understand it, but I could recognize the tender affection he'd always given her.

"Loved," he corrected, his gaze drifting to the ceiling. "That's what I have to figure out. The past tense of emotion."

I felt my anger toward her swell afresh. It had been less than three years. Had she ever loved him? I thought of Easton and my love. It could be volatile and insecure, but was always intense and present. Her cold withdrawal and Aaron's resigned acceptance was something I didn't understand.

I watched as he swallowed, the strong flex of his throat. "You'll find someone better."

He turned his head and looked at me. "I'm old, Elle. Too old to get back in the dating game."

"Hey," I protested. "You're the same age as me. You aren't allowed to call me old."

"Yeah, but you're beautiful." He smiled wryly, as if he'd been caught in the middle of stealing something. "You're the type of woman we all fall over ourselves to meet. I'm..." he searched for the right word. "Tired. Tired and heartbroken."

"Don't worry." I reached up and brushed his hair off his forehead, then stopped, the motion too intimate. "That can be an irresistible combination to some women. Tired and heartbroken is the most common search engine query among attractive women aged nineteen to thirty."

He laughed. "Okay, Elle Bell." He closed his eyes. "Thanks for trying to cheer me up."

The nickname was one he hadn't used in years, not since I would shack up at his and Easton's apartment, senior year. I almost teared up from nostalgia and leaned forward, wrapping my arms around him in a hug. "It'll be okay," I said softly. "I know it will."

We jumped apart when something hammered on the roof of the car and I looked over to see Chelsea jumping beside the door and rattling the handle. I unlocked the door and slid back to my place on the seat as she clambered in, followed by an exasperated Easton.

"Got it," she said cheerfully. "Though they made me spin on the pole to earn it back from the manager."

"Yeah, that wasn't how that happened," Easton responded, closing the door and pulling me onto his lap. "If I hadn't gone in, she'd still be on that pole."

Chelsea launched into her version of events and I knotted my fingers through Easton's, smiling when he lifted my hand up to his mouth and kissed it. Out of the corner of my eye, my gaze caught on Aaron who watched us, his own smile tinged in sadness.

I tried to catch his gaze, but he dropped his head back on the seat and closed his eyes, his arms crossing protectively over his chest.

13

LAS VEGAS POLICE INTAKE FORM
Name: Chelsea Pedicant
Offense: Indecency, Propositioning an Officer
Location: 3570 S Las Vegas Boulevard
Penalty: $500 fine and one night in jail

Report:

Ms. Pedicant approached cavalry officers stationed at the entrance to The Majestic on foot and appeared heavily intoxicated. She proceeded to hang onto Officer Stanton, who was also on foot. Upon being instructed to step back, she began attempting to disrobe from her wedding gown, but had trouble unfastening the back loops. Turning her back to Officer McGully, she asked for his assistance with the dress, then asked if he was "hung like his horse." Upon repeated commands to put her dress back on and move away from the officers, she was read her rights and then detained.

"This is your fault." I chucked a tater tot at Aaron's head from my spot on the hood. Swinging my legs gently, I watched as our limo driver lit up a cigarette on the far side of the police station. He hadn't seemed at all bothered by Chelsea's arrest, and maybe this was common-place in the city of sin.

"Hey, I told her to get directions from them." Aaron held up his palms in innocence. "I didn't ask her to start humping the guy's leg."

"She's referring to the part where you told Chelsea that cops counted double in the kiss count." Easton sat beside me, a cheese-burger in one hand, drink in the other.

I stole the soda from him and sucked on the straw. "Yeah. Plus, you knew what you were doing. Sending Chelsea over to a trio of uniforms is like putting cotton candy in front of kids." I had my own police fantasy, one I visited with frequent regularity, every time I sped through Coral Gables.

"Is there a reason you are in such a rush?" The officer would peer down at me, his gaze lingering on the open neck of my shirt, the top four buttons undone, my lace bra in full view.

My apologies and flustered explanations would be ignored, his expression getting sterner as he instructed me to step out of the car and move around to the passenger side, out of the view of the traffic. There, he'd tell me to put my hands on the roof of the car. He'd run his hands down my back and over my hips. He'd tell me to widen my stance and would sweep his hands up my bare legs and underneath my loose skirt. His breath would quicken when he realized I wasn't wearing any underwear. He'd run his hand in between my legs and swear when he discovered how wet I was. His hand would tighten on my shoulders and I would hear the indeci-sion in his silence as he warred between what he should do and what he wanted to do.

"Touch me again," I'd begged. "Please, officer. I need it so badly."

The fantasies typically took different paths from there. Sometimes he'd tell me that I was a dirty girl and needed to get on my knees and suck his cock. Other times he'd push his fingers inside of me, my face pressed against the cool side of my car, my mouth opening in a silent O of pleasure as he stood behind me, his hand furiously working between my legs. Sometimes he'd tell me to bend over the hood, and he'd unbutton his pants, and take me right there, the whip of passing cars drowning out my cries of pleasure.

Easton's hand settled on my knee and he squeezed it, then leaned in for a kiss. I allowed it, then flicked a piece of glitter off his neck with more force than needed. He winced and I smiled sweetly at him.

My phone dinged and I glanced down at the display. Calling Chelsea's father in the middle of the night had not been my first choice but, for once, the time zone had worked in our favor. Her 2 A.M. arrest happened around the same time that her father slipped into his cashmere robe and walked down the pearl-inlaid steps of his mansion. By the time I called, he was being served lobster Benedict and fresh-squeezed orange juice, the fruit picked from his own trees. He'd absorbed the information of Chelsea's arrest with a quiet chuckle, then asked for the location where she was being detained. He hung up with promises to get it handled. Now, $40 of cheap fast-food later, his message came through.

She is being released now. Please pick her up at the substation on Sierra Vista Drive.

I glanced at the street sign, verified our location, then texted him back to let him know we were already here.

Thank you, Elle. I appreciate your help.

He was really the coolest dad on the planet. Chelsea said that it didn't make up for her lack of a mother, but it wasn't for lack of trying. I loved my stiff and conservative parents, but if my friend ever called with news of my arrest, my dad would tell them to leave me in jail for an extra week, just to make sure I learned my lesson.

I pushed off the hood. "Daddy Warbucks said she's being released."

"Good." Aaron stretched. "I'm exhausted."

"Exhausted?" I teased him. "We had plans to visit a brothel next. Clean out those cobwebs that are hanging off of your dick."

"Ha." He picked up his McDonalds' bag and stuffed his trash into it. "I've got big plans to be asleep within the next hour."

"I think even Chelsea will agree with that plan."

As if on cue, the front door to the station opened and Chelsea wandered out, her hair half undone from her updo, her tiara stuck in the front cleavage of her dress like a pair of sunglasses. She saw us scattered along the limo and brought up her hands in touchdown stance, letting out a loud whoop of victory.

"Never boring," Easton reminded me as he helped me off the hood of the limo.

I smiled in response, then was pelted from the side as Chelsea tackled me in a perfume and beer-drenched hug.

Our suite was two master bedrooms. To avoid a Chelsea/Aaron sleeping arrangement, we'd put Chelsea and I in the left master, Aaron and Easton in the right. Between the two bedrooms was a sunken living room that boasted a sectional sofa, pool table, and fireplace. Our balcony overlooked the Strip and ran from one bedroom to the other. We didn't, much to Chelsea's chagrin, have a pool, though the website had shown one on the preview images when we'd booked the reservation.

I stepped into the suite and pulled off my shoes, feeling as if we'd been gone a week. Dropping my heels and my purse, I made it to the fridge and snatched a bottled water, trying not to think of its price as I broke the seal and chugged the water.

"I'm taking a shower," Chelsea announced. "Dibs on the right side of the bed."

"Let me run in there and use the bathroom really quick." I set down the water and headed to the lavish bath that was open to our room. Sitting on the toilet, I looked longingly at the deep soaker tub. Tomorrow I'd have to take an hour and enjoy that. Maybe when they headed down to the casino again.

"I'm so freakin' exhausted." Chelsea walked past me and stared in the mirror, examining her ruined updo. "Good lord, no wonder that cop turned me down. How long has my hair been like this?"

I wiped, then flushed the toilet. "Not until jail."

"Good." She wrestled her hand behind her back, struggling for the top clasp. "Can you undo this? I swear, next time I get a wedding dress, it's going to have a side zipper for easy access."

I quickly washed my hands at the sink, then went to work on the back of her dress, my fingers popping each of the fabric-wrapped buttons out of their closures. Getting to the bottom, I tugged on her zipper and laughed when I saw the nude granny panties she had on under the dress. "I can't believe you're wearing those."

"They're my chastity belt," she informed me, working the sleeves of the dress off. "To keep me from slutting it up. I wanted the focus to be on Aaron."

"Yeah, I'm not quite sure you accomplished that goal," I said dryly.

"Did he seem like he was thinking about Becca?" She winked at me.

I thought of that moment in the limo, the way he'd dropped his head back and sunk into the seat. In that private moment, yes. But for the most part, she was right. Her antics, and the city in general, had kept us all entertained.

"I'm going to tell E goodnight." I gave her a hug. "Don't snore too loudly tonight."

I left her grumbling and climbing out of her dress. Heading back to the kitchen, I closed the bedroom door behind me and caught Easton coming in from the hall. "Any luck?"

He lifted a small white shopping bag. "Concierge had some floss. Toothpaste too." He dropped the bag on the counter and glanced around the empty living room. "Everyone in bed?"

I watched one of his eyebrows cock and anticipated the suggestive grin, even before it spread over his lips. "I think they're taking showers. At least, I know Chelsea is."

He reached over and flipped the light switch by the door, the living room darkening. "How long do you think we have?"

I circled the pool table, coming around to his side of it and hoisting myself up and over its low edge. "Long enough." I reclined back, my elbows resting on the felt. "Ever fucked on a pool table, Mr. North?" The chandelier above the table was lit, a spotlight illuminating me, and I preened in its glow, opening my knees up to him.

He stopped before me and took his time unbuckling his belt and pulling it through the clasp. "You know I have."

I did. His fraternity house's chapter room had held a beer-spattered version, much crappier than this one. Before it made it to the dumpster, he'd screwed a fraternity brother's mom on it during Parent's Weekend. "I'd like the full Easton North billiard experience," I said softly, aware of our lack of privacy. "Assuming you can keep my voice down."

"Don't ask for something you don't want." He lifted his belt. "Open up, my filthy wife."

I didn't understand what he was referring to until his belt was at my mouth, the leather pushing flat against my tongue, my teeth digging into its edges. He cinched the belt tightly around my head and met my eyes. "Can you breathe?"

I nodded and tried to speak, my words muffled, the loss of speech strangely arousing. He leaned forward and put his mouth close to my ear. "Are you sure you want the full Easton North experience?"

I nodded and reached my foot out, rubbing it along the crotch of his slacks.

"Do you want me to fuck you like I fucked her?"

My affirmative cry was eaten by the leather, so I nodded again. Under the ball of my foot, his cock stiffened.

"It'll be harder than you like." He pulled at the spaghetti straps of my top, pulling the stretchy fabric down over my strapless bra. "I treated her like a whore and she loved it." He bent forward, his five o'clock shadow scraping against my shoulder, and undid my bra, tossing it to the side. He grabbed one of my exposed breasts, and his eyes met mine. "Nod if you understand."

I mocked him with my eyes.

He undid his fly and lowered his zipper, pushing away my foot as he withdrew his cock. "Nod if you understand."

My stern, stern husband. So bossy. So feral. I held his eye contact and nodded, my knees opening, and grinned around the gag as he pulled me to the edge of the table. Pulling my thong to one side, he positioned himself at my entrance. As I reclined further back on my elbows, I saw something on the balcony move.

I stiffened, my eyes narrowing in the space past Easton's shoulder, and in the moment before he thrust inside of me, I understood what it was. *Aaron.* He was standing on the balcony, his silhouette breaking the dotted landscape of lights. In between us there was a thick floor-to-ceiling wall of windows that blocked out the sound but would give him a clear view of everything that was happening.

My husband, still clothed, his dick jutting through his pants, his belt wrapped around my head.

My breasts hanging out, nipples hard in the suite's cool air, offered up as if for sacrifice.

The spotlight of the chandelier, shining down on me as he gripped my thighs and shoved inside of me.

I clutched at Easton's forearm, my nails digging in. He didn't react, his hold tightening on me as he started to thrust his hips in rapid concert, my body eagerly welcoming the intrusion. I could have told him. I could have reached back and undone the belt.

Pulled it out of my mouth. Let him know that we were on full display.

But I didn't. I didn't because knowing that Aaron was there, knowing that his eyes were on me, that his shadowy outline hadn't moved away from the view ... it was powerful. It bound my nerves in a way I'd never experienced before. I fell back against the felt and arched my back, squeezing and tugging on my breasts. I wrapped my legs around Easton's waist and urged him on, fucking him back as he drilled into me.

I *performed*, knowing that my husband's best friend was watching. Was Aaron's dick out? Was he stroking it? Was he watching my breasts jiggle from the impact and wanting to bury his face in between them? An inferno of arousal spread at the possibility that I had both of their attention, their arousal, their complete *need*.

The felt rubbed against my shoulders and Easton grunted, his eyes clamping on me, excitement burning through them. I looked down, between our bodies and felt dizzy seeing his swollen and wet cock, rigidly working in and out. Could he see the point of our connection? Could he see the tightening of my body as my orgasm approached? I stiffened when the peak came, arriving quicker and harder than any I'd ever had. Easton swore, clamping his hands on me to keep me in place, his furious pace unbroken as he continued through my orgasm.

When it finished, Easton pulled me into his arms and lowered me onto the floor. "I'm close," he gritted. "Get on your knees."

I did. My pussy flexing, clit tingling, my nipples aching for Aaron's mouth—I got on all fours, my head roughly yanked back as Easton pulled on the end of the belt. And there, even closer to the windows, my husband mounted and fucked me, plowing into me, over and over again, until I clawed against the thick rug, another orgasm peaking.

Was Aaron close? Was his hand as furious on his cock as Easton's was pumping inside me? This was it, as close as I'd ever come to my fantasies and it was *happening*, I was being fucked like a whore while my husband's best friend watched. It was happening, and I was loving every single moment of it.

The knowledge, the attention, the furious sounds and feel of my body being used—it all bundled into a twisted loop of pleasure, unfurling in a crescendo of pleasure that made my eyes roll back, my back flexing, a muted scream sounding against the dry taste of the leather. Easton felt it and leaned forward over my body, his hands framed on either side of mine, his chest against my back, and gave a soft roar, the sounds muffled in my hair, his body shuddering as he gave a few final thrusts and stopped.

My knees slid out and I relaxed onto my belly, afraid to look toward the window and see if Aaron was still there. Easton gently undid the belt and freed my mouth. Working my jaw open and closed, I smiled at the soft kiss he placed on my back.

"God, I fucking love you," he said quietly. "I didn't think we'd manage that without one of them coming out."

"I think Chelsea's in a coma," I rolled onto my back and repositioned my panties into place, hopeful that he wouldn't bring up Aaron. "How'd I compare with the Parent's Weekend mom?"

"No comparison." He gave me a long kiss, his mouth lingering as he took his time on the act. "You blow away every fantasy and prior experience I've ever had. It's kind of annoying, actually." He tucked his half-stiff cock back into his pants and left them unzipped.

"Oh really?" I teased, puffing up in pride as I pulled my top back over my breasts.

"Yeah. I'll be ruined if you ever leave me."

As if I ever could or would. I frowned. "I'd never leave you." I pulled him down for another kiss and looped my arms around his neck. "You're mine forever."

"In poorness and in wealth?" He smiled, but I saw the bit of fear in his eyes. We were the same, he and I. Both clinging to each other, both terrified of rejection. When had we lost our swagger?

Was it the normal evolution out of youth? He lifted me to my feet and I pressed a deeper, longer kiss onto his mouth.

"Forever," I repeated. "In everything."

He pulled me against his chest and I risked a glance out to the balcony, relieved to see that it was empty, no shadowy outline privy to this private moment.

14

I couldn't sleep. It was almost five in the morning Vegas time, eight in the morning back in Miami, and my mind would not stop spinning. Next to me, Chelsea—despite her assurances to the contrary—snored like a congested walrus. I rolled to my right side and tried to think of something—*anything*—other than Aaron standing at the window, watching us have sex.

My fantasies didn't use to be a problem. They sprung to force after I began fertility treatments, which is odd, since *low* libido had been one of dozens of the side effects that Dr. Rowe listed off. Maybe that was further proof that my body was rejecting the therapy, just like it rejected Easton's sperm and rejected my hopes for a family.

The digital display on the bedside clock flipped a minute higher, and I felt my anxiety spike with the change. What if I couldn't fall asleep at all? What if the men came in here at ten, ready for breakfast, and I was still red-eyed and wide-awake, scarred with the visual of what Aaron had seen?

Hadn't just seen, I reminded myself. *Watched.* He could have left. He could have realized that we were about to have sex and moved down on the balcony, out of sight. He could have given us our privacy but *he didn't*.

Why?

Maybe it was the curiosity of human nature. After all, I'd glanced in lit windows at night while walking Wayland. As he did his business, I'd watched the McDaniels argue in their kitchen, captivated by the secret glimpse into their lives. There had been something thrilling about seeing the personal moment between them when all pretenses were gone, shields down, the raw footage uncensored and unfiltered. Was this any different?

The truth was, if our neighbors hadn't been arguing—if Mr. McDaniel had instead been ripping open her blouse and bending her over their kitchen counter—I wouldn't have walked away. I would have stayed. I would have stood there, incredulous at what I was seeing, and stared. Maybe it would have turned me on. Maybe I would have wanted to join in.

Or maybe I was forcing my own desires into hypothetical Aaron's head because the major, major issue was that I had *liked* him watching. I had wanted to turn him on. I had wanted, and even expected, to have him open the balcony door and *join in*.

I rolled onto my back and stared at the ceiling. In the darkness of the room, I felt my fantasies stir. Beckoning. Seductive. Stronger. Weighted with actual possibility.

I pinned my eyes shut and focused on my breathing. Counting to one thousand, I imagined each number floating above my head, its digits dissolving in the darkness and replaced by the next. I fought, tooth and nail, against the images that slithered into my thoughts, stroked against my skin, pulsed inside my head.

Aaron beneath me, his mouth on my breast, his gaze on mine.

Easton behind me, my hair knotted in his grip, his finger tight in my ass.

Both of them, encouraging me. Worshipping me. Taking turns on me.

It couldn't happen. It was too close to real life. It was a fantasy that should have stayed in its place, behind the current of impossibility but there—in the City of Sin—I felt it bloom to life.

"I swear, I'd do filthy things to that waiter for a waffle right now." Chelsea leaned her head against Aaron's shoulder and eyed our chubby Korean server with longing.

"It's lunchtime. Wake up earlier tomorrow." He nudged her into place with his shoulder to keep her from falling off.

"Oh, right. Because you were up at dawn," she mumbled.

"Actually," he tilted his head. "I might have been up at dawn. I think I fell asleep around five."

I intently studied the French roll in my hand, tearing it in half and watching the bread pull apart. So I hadn't been the only one lying in bed, unable to sleep.

"Ugh. I was dead to the world as soon as I got out of the shower. I almost fell asleep in there." Chelsea lifted up a wrist heavy in David Yurman chains and glanced at her watch. "How long is our food going to take? I'm starrrrrving."

Easton's gaze found mine across the round table. I yawned, then winced, my cheek muscles still sore from his belt. His grin widened and I quickly shut my mouth. From beside Easton, I could feel Aaron watching, the heat from his gaze not helping the burn of my cheeks.

I stuffed part of the bread in my mouth and chewed.

"Hey." Chelsea straightened off Aaron's shoulder and leaned toward me. "I think I made a mistake with the cheeseburger. Want to swap?"

"No." I took a sip of lemonade to wash down the bread. "Order something else."

"Ellleee," she whined. "But then it'll take ages and I'm already SO hungry. Let me split your salad with you."

"I'll swap my steak for your burger," Aaron offered. She perked up at the prospect, and irritation bloomed in my chest.

"Don't trade her," I snapped. "She needs to learn to order what she wants." My gaze flipped to him and I was caught, full-force, in his eye contact. It was similar to when I once drove around a blind curve and encountered a deer. It froze, I inhaled, then I swerved and it ran away.

He knew. I lifted my glass of lemonade and rattled the ice, trying to get a piece in my mouth. *He knew that I saw him.* It was a sliver of possibility that felt as solid as a knife.

He knew and he knew I knew and *what the fuck* had I been thinking?

I suddenly felt hot, the sort of rapid overheating that comes right before you faint. I pressed the cold glass to my forehead and closed my eyes, focusing on taking short shallow breaths.

"Are you okay?" Chelsea was suddenly suction-cupped to my side, her breath on my shoulder, her hand biting into my arm. "Elle?"

I lifted my head before she freaked out and tried to smile. "I'm fine. Just hungover."

Dark melodic tones came from Aaron's cell, Becca's ringtone changed by Easton mid-flight into something from Star Wars that meant nothing to me. Aaron sighed and silenced the call. "She's called me more this weekend than she did all last month." As soon as Becca got word he was headed to Vegas, she'd gone full-court press in attempting to talk to him. Her ringtone had been an almost constant background noise, the chimes going off in the dinner buffet line, the suite, the limo, and in the strip club. We'd gotten a brief respite after Chelsea had answered, pretended to be a stripper, and then—in a mid-West accent that could curl off wallpaper—proceeded to tell Becca how hawt and dirty her future ex-husband was.

"Just answer it," Easton urged. "Find out what she wants."

My husband was too much of a romantic—his love of love

battling with his protectiveness toward his best friend. I could see the struggle in him, his advice often warring back and forth. Chelsea and I, on the other hand, were firmly on team Forget That Bitch. Aaron could do better. He deserved better. And as much as I hated the thought of divorce—at least she had filed before they had kids.

Aaron stood and palmed the phone. "I'll be back."

My anxiety dialed down as his tall frame walked toward the outdoor patio, his phone to his ear. I had the sudden urge to pull Easton to the side and tell him everything. He would know what to do and how to handle this. Because right now... it felt like I had done something wrong. And if Aaron *did* know that I *knew* he was on the balcony, then we were privy to something Easton wasn't. And that made my stomach knot with guilt.

"Are you constipated?" Chelsea leaned into me, her face pinched with worry. "You have that look on your face you get when you're constipated."

"No," Easton said slowly. "That's not her constipated face. That face is more of a wide lipped look." He imitated the face I supposedly make when my bowels are slow and I swore to God—constipation did not happen enough for me to have a dedicated facial expression.

I shoved Chelsea away from me. "Go away. I'm hungover. I told you. Your hovering is not helping."

"Oh, sir—that's mine." Chelsea zeroed in on the tuxedoed waiter right before he put Aaron's steak down at his empty place. "We switched. Give him the cheeseburger please."

He hesitated, then followed her instructions.

"I can't believe you're taking his steak."

"Whatever. I'm treating you guys to lunch so I'll order him another. Sir?" She batted her eyelashes at the waiter. "Can you put in another one for him?"

"Money doesn't solve everything, you know." I picked up my fork and stared at my Asian chicken salad, one selected because it was four dollars cheaper than anything else on the lunch menu.

"My, someone's soaked panties are in a twist this morning," Chelsea said airily. "You're in Vegas, dahling. With your deliciously scrumptious husband and lovable best friend. How are you *not* in a better mood right now? Would it help if all of my non-solvable money treated us both to a massage? I was thinking of getting a hot stone one."

A massage *would* help. So would a conversation with Easton, which seemed far more pressing than my slightly wilted salad. I gave Chelsea an apologetic look.

"What do you think she's saying to him?" Chelsea stuck a piece of steak in her mouth and half rose in her seat, trying to see outside. "I'm going to cut off his balls if he takes her back."

"He's not taking her back," Easton said, leaning back in his chair and draining his Pepsi. "We talked about it last night. Neither of us could sleep."

My awareness spiked. I tried to casually glance at Easton without rearing back like a stepped-on snake. "What'd you talk about?"

"I think she saw me. I had my dick out and was jacking off, and I could feel her looking at me, watching me.

"Did it turn you on, having my wife watch you?"

"Fuck, E—I wanted to open that door and join you. When she was on all fours, your belt in her mouth…"

"You should have. We could have taken turns on her. You won't believe her tight pussy, the way it clenches you. And she loves getting fucked, Aaron. You have no idea how dirty my wife can get."

I shifted in the seat, pushing my mound against the hard edge of the wooden chair. The ridge of it drug along my clit and if was socially acceptable, I'd hump this thing like an animal in heat.

"He's done with her. Emotionally finished." Easton droned on, oblivious to my fevered condition. "Especially with the way she's acting—which is completely dismissive about her actions. She hasn't apologized once, or seemed to care about his emotional well-being. Plus, he's checked their security cameras, and last night Becca never came home, so she must have stayed at that guy's place."

"The bitch," Chelsea said with almost gleeful pleasure. "I hope he throws her out on the street."

"Actually..." Easton frowned. "That house was built on her parent's land. Remember? That was their wedding gift to them?"

I forgot my rampant fantasy in the memory of what Aaron's sprawling house used to look like—an overgrown field on the outskirts of Miami. Their home had been Aaron's passion project —the gorgeous plantation home built between jobs, his weekends spent transforming the flat and swampy acreage. "What does that mean? Does that matter?"

"I don't know." Easton rubbed the back of his neck and bit into a potato wedge. "They're working through that and the business with a mediator. Neither one of them wants to get attorneys involved."

I hated the thought that all of his hard work on that house could go to her.

E hunched forward over his plate. "His mom came back this weekend. I told him he could move in with us until he figured his shit out."

His words hovered in the air above the table. I chewed slowly, a sour tangerine popping on my tongue. *Stay with us?* No. No. NoNo-NoNo *No*.

"But..." I set down my fork. "Maybe he *needs* his mom's support. It's a tough time for him. Plus, I have all of that Christmas stuff in the guest room. It's a lot of stuff..." I ended weakly. Easton tilted his head at me as if I'd gone insane. Even Chelsea lifted her attention from her food.

"I can move it to the garage. That's where it should be anyway. And you've met Mama D." He didn't have to elaborate. I had met Mama D. I'd met her, been crushed in a hug by her, and left her house ten minutes later with enough advice to write a book, and two Tupperware containers full of food. She was well-intentioned, but had the subtlety and boundaries of Dr.Phil on acid. "Do you have an issue with him staying with us?"

"Of course not. Why would I?" I sent out a silent plea to the universe to send me back a well-thought-out and perfectly reasonable excuse why Easton's best friend couldn't shack at our place while his life fell apart.

No such excuse came. I stuffed another forkful of salad into my mouth and chomped through it.

"It looks like they can fit us in at three-thirty," Chelsea announced, looking up from her phone. "Easton, you and Aaron want in on massages too?"

"Nah, I think we'll stick to the tables." Easton leaned forward and tapped my hand, getting my attention. "If you don't want him to stay with us, just let me know."

I was acutely aware of Chelsea, the hum of the neighboring tables, and Aaron approaching quickly from the left. I forced a smile and met Easton's eyes. "No, it's fine. Seriously." In my stomach, the bits of chicken and lettuce churned as anxiety grew.

Anxiety... and something else. I took a sip of water and placed a hand on my stomach, trying to place the discomfort and hoping like hell that it wasn't excitement.

15

There are some things your husband should never know. My mother's words echoed in my mind as I watched Easton pull open the sliding glass door and step onto the balcony, joining Aaron at the rail. Together, they looked over the Vegas view, and I felt a pull of longing at how handsome they both were. Easton turned to Aaron and laughed, his hand clapping on his shoulder with affection.

Would last night's events drive a wedge between the two friends? Would Easton be mad?

I had no idea. I also didn't know how much to tell Easton when that moment of truth came. There was a difference between knowing that someone was watching and *performing* for them.

The two men moved closer, and Aaron leaned his forearms on the rail. I thought of the time when Easton had shoulder surgery and A fell asleep in the recliner in his hospital room and stayed the night. There had been the night he showed up at our house, an hour after he heard about Easton's skull fracture, a case of beer in hand. We'd all gotten drunk that night, and I'd woken up to find our abandoned bedroom dresser assembled—a Herculean task that had endeared me to him forever.

It shouldn't matter if my overactive imagination dabbled in explicit Aaron fantasies. Or if—in a lonely and drunk moment—he watched us have sex. I couldn't throw a wrecking ball into their friendship.

But I also couldn't not tell Easton.

"Whatcha doing?"

I jumped at the close sound of Chelsea's voice, turning sharply to see her standing beside me, her arms crossed over her generous chest. Jutting out from her hot pink cut-off shorts, her legs were planted wide, as if she was about to go into a series of squats.

"I was just blanking out. Thinking about work."

"Any word on your contract negotiations?"

"The buyers are still thinking about it," I lied. In actuality, the doomed inspection hadn't killed the deal after all. The buyers had accepted our proposed repairs and we had only had to bump closing for two weeks—still a little financially spincter-tightening, but not wrinkle-inducing.

"No wonder you've been so quiet." She leaned forward and draped her weight on my shoulders. "You've been off all morning."

I made a face. "It's almost three. I think we missed morning entirely."

"Uh-huh," she said, not distracted from her assessment of me. "Well, you're allowed to be grouchy for thirty more minutes. Then I expect this massage to melt all of that away. We've got Luke and Thomas booked, and the concierge told me they have magic fingers and fart out sex appeal."

I watched as she stretched forward to touch her toes, which was probably the extent of the physical activity she had planned for the week. "Really? That's what the concierge said?"

"In snooty old lady talk which, thanks to Regina, I'm fluent in." The reference to her stepmother was made with a groan, as she struggled to reach her toes, then hefted upright. "I'm starting yoga," she announced. "Tuesdays and Thursdays at ten, at that place that likes to microwave you while you downward dog. You in?"

"As tempting as that offer is, no." I did my own mini stretch out of obligation, knotting my hands behind my back and attempting to expand the tight muscles in my chest. I glanced back at the balcony, where Easton had turned, his back now against the railing, attention still on Aaron.

We should head downstairs now, before I had to suffer through another awkward round of interactions. Easton had already asked me once if everything was okay. I couldn't bear delivering another forced assurance, when all I really wanted was to get him back at our house and talk to him alone.

But when could I do that? Based on the tail end of our lunch conversation, Aaron was moving his personal items out tomorrow. We'd bumped up our flight plan to get him into Miami early enough to go home and pack. My helpful husband would be right there, running interference on Becca while shoveling Aaron's stuff in garbage bags and cardboard boxes.

By the time Easton finally got home, he'd have Aaron in tow. They'd want to eat and watch baseball. I wouldn't be able to—

"Hey." Chelsea gently bumped me with her shoulder. "Are you coming? It's time to head down to the spa."

I grabbed my bag and turned away from the view. "Yeah, I'm ready."

As terrifying as it was, I needed to have this conversation with Easton *here* in Vegas, so I could kill all of this now, before the three of us headed back to Florida as roommates.

I cornered my husband between an Aladdin slot machine and an anorexic millennial with blue hair and a nose ring. "We need to talk." I claimed the machine next to him and stuck my room key in.

Easton glanced over, half-distracted by the still-spinning reels. "What's wrong?"

The machine displayed my points total, then wished me good luck. "Face forward and act normally."

"Did you win something? The Wheel of Fortune jackpot?" He crowded me, his voice rising, and I made a mental note that—if I ever *did* win—he had a horrible poker face.

"Chill out, we didn't win anything. Where's Aaron?" I fed a five-dollar bill into the machine and kept my face mild, in case he was lurking around the corner and watching us.

"Cleaning up at blackjack." He jerked his head toward the table games and I abandoned my act at the news that we were alone.

"Good." I pushed my left sleeve up over my elbow, then the right. "I need to tell you something but I don't want you to freak out or get weird about it."

He eyed me warily. "Okay."

"Last night, when you and I were in the living room—" I paused. "Aaron…" I took a deep breath. "I think Aaron was on the balcony."

The millennial groaned, yanked her card out of the machine and stood to leave. I took the excuse to look away from Easton.

"He told me."

The three words brought me back. "Aaron told you?"

"Yeah." He rubbed the back of his neck and gave a wry smile. "I was actually struggling with how to tell *you*." He chuckled. "So, look—problem solved."

No, the problem wasn't solved. Not at all. I moved closer to him and lowered my voice, conscious of the fact that we were in a very public place. "So he told you that he watched us? Watched you… gag and fuck me?"

"Well, I'm not sure that *watched* us was the word he used. But that he saw us, yeah."

"And?" I watched his face for tells. His features were relaxed, his eyes amused, and I didn't see any of the stress that was pinching my shoulder blades with an iron grip. Even the massage hadn't helped, though the man had been given an extra ten bucks in his tip for trying really, *really* hard.

He shrugged. "And what?"

I blew out an irritated breath. "This is a big deal, Easton. He could have moved down the balcony and gone into your room, but he didn't." *I could have pulled out the gag and told you, but I didn't.* I almost said it, almost put the spotlight on me just to knock that relaxed smirk off his face.

"You're right." His face sobered and he moved closer. "I'm sorry. He was drunk and the door to our bedroom was locked. But still, he could have banged on the window. I'll have him apologize to you."

"What? No. NO. Don't have him do that." I shook my head emphatically and added my hands into the mix, my alarm causing my voice to pitch at an unreasonably high level.

"Okay..." he said slowly. "I'm confused. What do you want me to do?"

"I want...." I faltered, unsure. I wanted to be honest with him. I wanted things to be open and forthright between us. I didn't really want him to know that I harbored secret fantasies of an Easton and Aaron sandwich, but was suddenly terrified of the idea of him coming to live with us. What if I couldn't handle it? What if I was gasping against the kitchen counter, my hand deep in my panties, mid-fantasy, and Aaron caught me?

I'm not responsible for the things that happen in my own home. It was supposed to be my safe haven. My erogenous zone. I was an addict, and putting Aaron in our house was paramount to stocking an alcoholic's cupboards with Grey Goose. I might dust around those bottles for a week or so, but I'd be chugging from the bottle in a vomit-covered T-shirt before long.

I *would*. And if he was standing there, watching us last night ... maybe he would too.

I clutched at Easton's arm and tried to find the right words. "I don't know if I want him to stay with us."

"What?" He stepped back enough to properly focus on my face. "Because of last night? Elle, we were all so drunk last night, I don't think he even remembers what he saw. You can't—" he inhaled. "Elle."

"It's not just that he saw us. It's that I liked it." There. It was there, I said it, and I watched it like a burning fuse, bracing myself for the resulting explosion.

"You liked what?" He understood, he had to understand, yet he played dumb, his handsome features scrunching in thought as if I'd just fed him an algebraic equation.

"Don't be dense." I crossed my arms and gave him an annoyed glare. "I knew he was watching us fuck and I *liked* it."

"Umm..." The blue-haired girl cleared her throat and I turned to find her right behind me, one black fingernail pointed toward her slot machine. "I left my drink there."

I moved to one side and watched as she eased by us and picked up her clear cup. "Freaks," she muttered.

Easton waited as she ambled away at the slowest pace possible, sucking loudly on her straw. He followed her movement, then flicked those baby blue eyes back to me.

He was aroused. He was trying to hide it, but it was telegraphed in the hungry way he moved closer, the strong pinch of his forehead, the way he attempted to compose himself before he spoke. "And that's why you don't want to let him live with us? Your voyeuristic tendencies aren't exactly a surprise, Elle. After all..." he checked the area for more ears. "Remember—"

I held up my palm. "I don't need a recap of every time I've assaulted you in public. I blame most of those on tequila." *And how incredibly hot Easton was.* My fantasy partners always paled in comparison to what he could do with just one cocky tilt of his mouth.

"Most." His hand closed tenderly around mine. "But not all."

I didn't respond, not when he softly kissed my cheek, then just beside my mouth, then the tip of my nose. His chest brushed against mine and I inhaled the subtle scent of his blackberries and beach cologne. "You're trying to distract me," I said, in the moment before his soft lips landed on mine.

"Is it working?"

"No." I pulled away and sat on the closest padded stool. "This is serious, E."

He sighed. "It's not a big deal. He saw us together. You like public sex. We move on."

"I've never had public sex where someone actually saw us. Not that close, and certainly not..." I pointed to my mouth and made a face as if I still had the gag in it. Our rare moments of public indecency had been the sort of quickies in public that might have been suspected but not confirmed—a blow job in the back stacks of the library, sex in the backyard in the middle of the day, a finger session on a transatlantic flight where I bit into a neck pillow to stifle my groans.

"I already told him he could stay. It's going to be fucking awkward if I tell him he can't now. Plus, where's he gonna go? Back to his mom's?"

"He could get a hotel," I said, then realized how sullen I sounded.

Easton sighed. "Come on, Elle. Work with me here. If you're uncomfortable around him, then I'll keep you guys apart. But it's Aaron. You love him. I don't know why you're acting like everything has suddenly changed."

Maybe I *was* blowing this out of proportion. I'd lived with them before, for two weeks when I'd been in between apartments. It'd been fine. Unremarkable. A little annoying, their bromance one that sometimes made me feel like a third wheel. But fine. I could do it again.

He kissed the top of my head. "Are we good?"

"Yeah." I looked down at the Aladdin slot machine, where 14

credits remained. Reaching out, I hit the Max Bet button and watched as the dials spun. Aladdin, Jasmine, and Jafar lined up in uneven formation, the omen eerie with its timing.

"Come on." Easton slung an arm around my shoulders and pulled me onto my feet. "Let's find the others and get something to eat."

16

After the dry Vegas heat, Miami felt like an oven set to steam. My shoes still on, I laid on the top of the covers and listened to the drone of the lawnmower. On a normal day, I might have stood at the window and watched the man, admiring the way his shirt clung to his muscular back, his strong legs churning against the freshly cut grass as he pushed the walking mower.

Now, I didn't have time for a fantasy about my sexy landscaper. I had bigger issues, which were currently occupying both ends of our living room couch, their feet kicked up on the ottoman, beers in hand, their eyes glued to the TV, masculinity reeking off them and infecting the room.

I'd popped the cap off my own beer and joined them, drawn forward by the familiar sound of the game. I'd avoided the couch and settled back in the big red leather recliner, tucking my feet underneath me and staring at the screen.

I'd lasted ten minutes before I'd realized that Aaron was studiously ignoring me. Every comment I made, every glance I shot over—he was polite and engaged in the game, but stiff as a board around me.

I hated it and left the room, making an excuse about needing a shower.

From the direction of the living room, dual shouts rang out. Easton yelled something at the top of his lungs. I shifted onto my side and wondered what had happened.

This was ridiculous, me in our bedroom, hiding out like a leper. I tilted my head toward the closet door and considered changing into something nice and going out. The realtors in our office were having a wine and cheese event at a downtown bar. I could join them, though the idea of hobnobbing with that many botox-enhanced foreheads sounded exhausting. Plus, I had no new contracts. No new listings. No achievements to casually drop while everyone else rattled theirs off under the guise of shop talk. My gaze drifted to the tall suitcase, parked by the closet door where it had sat for the last two days. We would both ignore it, avoiding the gold Samsonite until the dire moment when Easton needed his electric razor, or I wanted my red sling-backs.

The door handle jiggled and I turned as the heavy brass lever turned. The door eased open and Easton stuck his head in. "Hey. Halftime just started. Did you already get a shower?"

"Not yet." I rolled toward him and sat up. "I didn't want to do it with Luke in the backyard, given the broken blinds." I nodded in the direction of the backyard, where the weed-eater roared to life. "It's almost dark. Why's he here so late?"

"No idea." He looked at our bathroom blinds, which were stacked next to the dresser, needing to be taken to the trash can. They were on the same wait-until-the-other-person-does-it schedule that our suitcase was, and in tattered shreds thanks to an enthusiastic attempt by Wayland to catch a moth. "Want me to have him stop? Aaron and I can finish up whatever he hasn't gotten to."

"No." I stood up and stretched. "I think I'll change and go to the gym. What's the score?"

"Tied." He watched as I worked open the buttons on my shirt.

"Aaron's running over to Bobalo's to pick up a pizza. So..." He maneuvered around the blinds and tugged at my shirt, pulling me closer to him.

I let out a strangled laugh at the suggestive grin on his face. "Now?"

"Come on." His hand fumbled at the button of my long shorts. "It'll take him a half hour, given that construction on Fourth. Plus, I ordered a deep dish, just to give us extra time."

"Oooh... deep dish." I stuck the tip of my tongue barely out at him. "That was assumptive. What if I wasn't in the mood?"

"My wife?" He smirked. "She's always in the mood."

If I hadn't been before, that phrase right there did it for me. I liked the idea of him being married, and the hypothetical scenario of me being his other woman. "Would she share you with me?" I gripped him through his jeans, enjoying the hiss of caution that he let out.

"Fuck no. She'd be furious if she knew what I was about to do to you." He roughly kissed my neck as he yanked my shorts over my wide hips, his actions competing with mine as we both struggled to get the other's clothes off. We kissed, his mouth possessive, and I shivered as my shirt fell away, my skin breaking out in goosebumps in the cold room.

"You know, my wife gives one hell of a blow job." He palmed my breasts in each warm hand and squeezed. "Think you can do better?"

"Ha." I pushed him onto the bed and straddled him. "I dole out blowjobs after orgasms. Get me to five, and I'll suck your dick so hard you'll leave your wife for me."

"Yes ma'am." He sat upright and grinned up at me, his hands caressing over my nipples as his dick twitched against my ass. I raised up on my knees and reached down, positioning him between my legs. His hands tightened on me in warning. "Wait, the door."

I glanced over my shoulder at the door, which hadn't fully closed behind him. "It's fine." I lowered myself onto him, sighing in contentment as his thick cock pushed into me. So hard, so quickly. It had been one of the rumors at Florida State, proved true and still accurate, seven years later.

"You like it open?" The question hissed through his lips right before he reclaimed my mouth, his hand wrapping through my hair and tugging on it. "You hoping he'll come home early and see you riding my cock?"

I hesitated in the middle of my action, his cock halfway in, and met his gaze. It was intense and possessive, his grip on me fierce, his dick rigid. If he was mad, it was the hottest version of the emotion I'd ever seen. He jerked his hips underneath me, jabbing deeper. I came down fully. "Maybe."

"Fuck maybe," he swore, his hands running up my thighs and gripping my ass, pulling my cheeks apart as one of his fingers found the pucker of my ass. "Tell me. Tell me you want him to see this beautiful ass riding up and down my cock."

My nails dug into his chest as I spoke, caution thrown to the wind, the risk as hot as the pleasure. "I want him to see it."

"Do you?" he gritted out, his finger pushing into the tight pucker of my ass. "You know he won't just stand there. Not when he sees how fucking dirty you are. Not when he hears how you sound when you take my cock." He pulled me down to his chest and trapped me in place, holding me still as he took over the motion, his hips beginning a furious assault of upward thrusts into my needy body. He turned his head and put his mouth close to my ear. "Is that what you want, Elle? Do you want him to come into our bedroom? Do you want to see his cock? You know he's going to be rock hard, seeing what he's about to fuck."

I broke at the visual, clutching his shoulders and letting out a howl of pleasure as his second finger pushed into my ass, the fit tight and dirty and hot, my muscles spasming around him as my orgasm pulsed.

His fingers yanked out and he rolled, getting on top of me. "Flip over," he ordered. "On your knees."

I scrambled up the bed, obeying him, the lilac comforter bunching under my knees. He pulled them outward, spreading me wide, and pushed my shoulders down until my breasts brushed the bed. "Stay right there. Arch your back."

The bed shifted and I paused, tilting my head to one side. The weight of his steps sounded as he moved to the side. His belt clanked against the wood floors and I saw him hold up his phone. "What are you doing?"

"Stay there." There was the sound of a shutter and I flinched.

"Why are you—"

He gripped a fistful of ass and squeezed, then spanked the flesh, almost lifting me off the bed. "You're so fucking beautiful. I want you to see this." There was another shutter sound, then the phone was tossed beside me, screen side up, and as Easton got behind me, I saw what he had taken. It was the sort of trashy picture you'd see on an amateur porn site. My legs split wide, my pussy pink and glistening, back arched, face turned away, my toes braced on the bed. His fingers were biting into my ass cheek and his stiff cock was visible in the bottom half of the frame, wet from being inside me.

He pushed in, and I closed my eyes at the rigid fill of him, the photo disappearing for one pleasurable moment. "That's what he's going to see," Easton began to pump into me, his pelvis slapping loudly against my ass. "He's going to hear you crying out for more and he's going to walk down the hall and see the cracked door. He's going to get hard at the sound of you coming. He's going to look in, and he's going to see you—just like that."

I gripped the sheets tighter and imagined Aaron at the door, his weight braced against the jamb, his mouth half open as he took in the scene.

"Look how fucking gorgeous you are." Easton tightened his grip on my waist, his strokes shortening as his speed increased, his arousal growing.

Staring down at my husband's phone, I let myself look at it

without focusing on the dimples of my ass, or my unshaved bikini line. I listened to the growl of his voice, felt the urgency of his fucks, and looked at the pure fucking hotness of the photo. I did look gorgeous. I looked needy, Easton looked huge, and I felt drunk at the thought of Aaron seeing that view. Drunk and reckless.

"Talk to me, baby." Easton spread my cheeks with his hands, the cool air of the room hitting the exposed pucker of my ass. "Tell me what you want."

I couldn't answer that, could barely manage a moan of pleasure as my muscles knotted and tightened around his cock. I managed an exhale. "More."

He withdrew and I felt the hot swipe of his tongue along the crack of my ass, then the push of it against the tight band of nerve endings. "Nooo..." I warned. "I'm not ready."

"I fucking need it, Elle." He pushed his thumb into my ass and my clit tingled, a shot of pleasure shooting from one nerve center to the other, my body humming like an electric wire in preparation. "Please. I'll fucking come the moment I push inside."

That was a lie. He loved my ass too much to be quick. But I also craved the way he reacted when he was inside of it. The filthy things he said. The fierce possession that came over him. The raw, unfiltered and animalistic joining of our bodies and how intimate and fierce the connection was.

I felt the wedge of another finger, prying me open.

"Come on. Please." His dick bumped against my swollen clit, the head of it pushing insistently against everything it touched. He leaned forward and bit my right shoulder blade. "Or are you worried you'll be too loud?" He put the head of it against the tight opening. "Are you worried he'll hear you beg for more?"

Fuck it. I pushed back against his head, mewing in pain as my ass stretched to take him, my clit engorging, heavy with need. I reached between my legs and brushed my hand over the sensitive bud, gently strumming over the wet folds, the needed pleasure bringing tears to my eyes. "Slowly," I whispered.

"Jesus Christ," he muttered. "It's so hot and tight. It feels insane." He leaned forward and cupped my breasts, his damp palms rolling over my nipples, and he gave mini thrusts of his hips as he eased deeper inside of me, the pinch of one nipple distracting me from the pain.

"Use your fingers," he urged. "Play with that beautiful pussy and pretend it's his tongue."

I couldn't. The orgasm was too blinding, too intense, too unexpectedly sudden and I rocked back, impaling him on me, his grunt of pleasure breaking the last tie of control. I screamed, my body quaking, and he gripped my shoulders, moving his slick cock in and out of my tight ass. I screamed again, my orgasm spurred on by the reckless volume, the belief that Aaron might hear, he could know, he could be standing at the dark crack of the door and watching as Easton took my ass and fucked me through this orgasm.

"I'm gonna come." Easton's hand tightened on my shoulder and he swore, gasping as his hips slowed, his pleasure peaking, and he called out my name, a cry of worship in the moment before he collapsed to one side of the bed and pulled me with him.

We laid there under the slow swipe of the fan in sated silence. He moved, his dick sliding out of me, and I winced at the spark of discomfort.

"Fuck," he drawled. "You are insane, you know that?" He pulled me into his chest and I laid my head against his head, the rapid heartbeats tapering off into a more peaceful rhythm. Reaching over, he tugged at the sheet, draping it over my naked body, protecting the view. A long moment passed and I listened to the sounds of the house. From down the hall, the television was barely audible. The yard was quiet, and I suddenly thought of the landscaper.

"How much of that do you think the yard guy heard?"

"He probably can't hear shit after listening to that mower for the last hour. Don't worry about it." He twisted a dark lock of my hair around his finger and gently tugged. "Let me get the door."

I propped up on one elbow and watched as he made it to the door and shut it, working the door into the frame. He kicked it with his foot and it knocked into place. When we moved in, our neighbors told us that Hurricane Donna picked our house up a little, then set it back down. I didn't know if I believed that story, but it would explain why it doesn't seem to have a single right angle. Coming back to the bed, I watched as he lowered his naked body beside me.

"This is interesting." He used his forefinger to move a fallen chunk of hair out of my eyes. Snagging his finger on a bobby pin, he carefully removed the offending item, then tossed it in the general direction of the bathroom. "This Aaron fascination you suddenly have."

"I wouldn't call it a fascination." I frowned. "You're the one who just took all of that there."

"You seemed to like it." His finger ran across my collarbone and pulled at the sheet, dragging it down until my breasts were exposed. Reverently, he caressed the twin mounds. They were one of his favorite parts of my body. I had a brief moment of vanity, thinking of what pregnancy would do to them. Maybe my stubborn uterus was for the best. Maybe, with all of the torrid thoughts in my head—I wasn't fit to be a mom anyway.

"Did you?" Easton dropped his head and took the closest nipple into his mouth, tenderly sucking at the sensitive bud.

I sighed and cupped the back of his head, watching. "I did like it."

"Have you ever thought about him before?" His gaze flicked up to meet mine, but he kept his mouth in place, the scruff of his beard brushing over the delicate curve of my breast.

"Before Vegas?" I hesitated. "Sometimes. But never just him. I would think about him and you, doing stuff with me."

He lifted his mouth. "Really?" He frowned, considering the

idea. "Both of us with you at the same time? Like double penetration?"

"No, no, no." I made a face at the idea. "Like, other stuff. I don't know. Stupid stuff."

He moved higher up on the bed until our faces were level. "Tell me."

"Noooo." I kicked a leg out from under the sheet, freeing it.

"Come on." He inched closer until his mouth was inches away, the warm blow of his breath against my lips. "Tell me."

"Easton…" I tried to pull back and his mouth captured mine, his hand cupping my head and pulling me to him. I struggled against his kiss, keeping my lips stiff, my tongue unresponsive.

"Stop fighting me," he whispered, gently pressing small pecks against my lips before trying again for a deeper kiss.

I gave in, relaxing into his touch as my mind churned through his questions. *Have you ever thought about him before? Tell me.* It wasn't like Aaron was the crux of my fantasies. I'd had so many unwelcome thoughts about so many men—Aaron just happened to be the one who I was currently literally tripping over, the one who had stood on that dark balcony and made my first fantasy come to life. If I was start confessing my thoughts to Easton, maybe I should bring up my secret scenarios about someone else, someone who wasn't in our house, eating dinner with us every night. Someone who didn't feel so close.

Someone who didn't feel like an actual possibility.

Because he wasn't, right? Everything Easton just said, that roleplay we just did…

"I didn't mean all of that." I broke away from the kiss, looking up to the ceiling as he planted kisses on my neck, then collarbone. "I was just role-playing."

His hand traveled down the bare length of my body, and I let out a moan as his fingers dipped in between my legs, my folds slick, his entry wet. "Are you sure?" He turned his head, watching his glistening fingers as they pushed in, then withdrew.

In, then out. My pelvis tilted up on its own accord, begging for more. "Because you seemed like you did." He turned, his gaze pinning on mine. "Tell me what you had thought about. With Aaron."

I sucked in a breath, aware that this was an unnecessary relationship risk, only moderately justified by the dark look of arousal on his face, the seductive play of his fingers as they hypnotically pulsed in and out of me. Had I ever seen such intensity on his features? Such need? Maybe at the beginning. Maybe during those lust-filled early nights. But not in a long time, even with the fireworks show that our sex often became.

I parted my legs wider, my thighs beginning to tremble. "Just, being between the two of you. On my knees."

His gaze darkened, his eyes hooding as his fingers pressed deeper, curving up to scrape along my G-spot. I arched halfway off the bed. He nodded. "Keep going."

"That's it."

"You aren't a good liar, my sweet wife." He rubbed his forefinger along my inner ridge and I began to pant, my pelvis twitching in response to his touch. "Keep going."

"Someone behind me," I gasp. "Not necessarily him. Just someone. While you make me suck your cock." I twisted on top of the sheets, frantic to get to the orgasm. He eased his fingers a torturous inch or so out, then did something that felt like pure heaven.

"I like the thought of competing over you." He placed a hand on my chest and pressed, pinning me down. "I like the idea of seeing the look on your face when someone other than me pushes inside of you." He continued the motion and I clawed along a pillow, my eyes pinching shut as I flexed every muscle in my body and then broke.

Waves. Glorious waves of pleasure. I moaned his name as I shuddered, my body curling around his hand, my sensitivity growing as the orgasm faded, his touch softened. I exhaled and relaxed, one foot twitching as a last tendril of pleasure uncurled. I opened my eyes and found him watching me.

"But I don't think I could let someone else have you," he said gruffly, leaning forward until his face was just above mine. He brushed a tender kiss on my left cheek, then my right. "I think I'd kill anyone who touched you, no matter how fucking hard I get at what you just said."

I met his third kiss with my lips and smiled against the touch. "I'm good with that."

"Are you sure?" He carefully brushed my hair away from my face, then cradled my chin, studying me. From the front to the house, a door slammed and Wayland gave a series of loud barks, then fell silent. Chances were that Aaron, with a pizza in hand, was being attacked from a dog with an addiction to anything involving cheese, bread, or meat.

"They were just thoughts," I said. "Thoughts that terrify me."

"In what way?"

"What they might do to us."

He kissed me again, then rolled off the bed and stood, the muscles in his body precisely outlined. Four years out from playing, he was still a perfect athletic specimen. His dick, big and beautiful, jutting out from between those strong thighs. His blond hair, rough from my fingers, that sunburnt nose and handsome features, with eyes that gleamed with sexual promise. There were times I saw insecurity in Easton—discussing our finances, on his way to important meetings—but in the bedroom, he'd always been confident. Naked, his cockiness was at an all-time. I studied the lines and cuts of his body and tried to imagine how I'd feel if he said those same things to me.

That he was fantasizing about another woman. Multiple other women.

That he was turned on by the thought of them in our bed.

That he wanted to fuck them while I used his mouth.

I'd have stormed out of bed, pulled on my clothes, and packed a bag. I held my breath, tensing as Easton reached down and picked up his jeans. Skipping his underwear, he pulled one leg on and then the other. Palming his dick, he grimaced as he pushed it down and into the tight fit of his jeans.

I studied the level of his erection. "Did you take something?"

He stopped his efforts and gave me an exasperated look. "Really? Have I ever needed to take anything?"

"I'm just asking because of the last time." The 'last time' was the one and only time he took a Cialis. A guy on the team had passed him the pill, one which had produced immediate and impressive results that lasted seven hours, despite him having three orgasms and a lot of concerned deflation efforts on our part. I'd wanted to call the ER, he had staunchly refused, and we'd had ice packs on and the team doctor on call by the time it finally started to wilt.

"Nope. This is all you." He stretched out a white Hanes T-shirt and pulled it over his head. Bending over the bed, he gave me another kiss. "I love you."

"Love you too." I pulled the sheet back over me, and watched as he zipped up his pants. His gorgeous features winced as he fastened the button. "Are you sure that's going to go down?"

"Any minute." He came forward and sat on the edge of the bed and I tensed. Maybe this was it. The moment of the fight. A cumulation of the Vegas and mid-sex confessions.

Twisting toward me, he leaned across my stomach, his weight pulling the sheet tightly against my breasts. I shifted, and he put the bulk of his heft on his elbow. "You can tell me the truth, Elle. About what you want."

I wanted to say the same thing to him, given that his dick was about to pierce a hole through the front of his jeans. Maybe the idea of me being with someone else did make him furious, but it also, most definitely, turned my husband on.

He was waiting, and I tried to figure out what I *truly* wanted. An open marriage? Hell no. A threesome? Maybe. *Yes.* Maybe. "I don't know what I want," I said finally. "I think the fertility drugs are knocking my hormones all out of whack. It isn't just Aaron. I've been thinking about a lot of men."

It felt wrong to blame the fertility drugs, yet they had been what had brought all of this on. Prior to those drugs, I had a perfectly normal, if not slightly over-active libido, one fully centered on my husband.

He didn't react, his palm brushing over the top of the sheet and awakening one pert nipple. "What men?"

I winced. "A lot of different ones. Too many to list. Honestly, it's embarrassing."

He stilled. "Dr. Jenthric?"

A laugh burst unexpectedly out of me. "What?! No. He's like ninety!"

"Your boss? Please don't say so. I know that's a common fantasy among women." He looked almost serious enough to sell the question, if you missed the playful twinkle in his eye.

I grabbed a pillow and swung it at his head. "I hate you. Be serious for one moment. I'm not talking about bald gay men or old pediatricians."

He dodged a second swing of the pillow, stole it from me, and tossed it to the side. Grabbing my wrists, he pinned them to the bed on either side of my head. "How worried should I be about these fantasies?"

"Not worried," I said honestly. "They've been going on ever since we started trying to get pregnant, and I haven't done anything with anyone."

"But this is why you didn't want Aaron to stay with us?" He studied me from his dominant position, then eased his weight off my wrists, freeing them.

I immediately reached for his hair, threading my hands through the thick strands. "All of my other fantasies were with people I have little to no contact with. It just seems too close, having him right here. What if I mess up?"

"Mess up? You won't." It was scary, how much my husband trusted me. The clear faith on his face, the absolute confidence that I would never step over the line with his friend. He leaned down and brushed his lips over mine. "You won't. You're too good for that and we're too strong for that."

It was quite possibly the most reckless thing any spouse could think, let alone say. I knew we were strong. I had no interest in actually attempting any of my fantasies, but I was still freaked out by the idea that Aaron was staying with us and Easton had engaged in a role-play that involved him.

Steps sounded down the long hall, then paused outside our door. There was a rap of knuckles. "E? Game's back on."

"Coming," Easton called out, then pushed to his feet. "Talk about this later?"

"Sure." *Please, no.* We needed to put this conversation and his last remaining Hawaiian shirt in a wooden box, bury it in a deep hole, then run like hell. These were not the talks that successful marriages were built on. These were the sort of talks that led to danger, the kind of confessions that later, when reviewing divorce paperwork, everyone regretted.

He gave me a kiss and it felt like a promise of something. "Come out and eat?"

"I'm going to take a shower. Wash all of you off of me," I teased, and it came out right. Light and fun, void of the dark pit that had settled in my stomach at the thought of leaving our bedroom and facing Aaron, after everything I just envisioned. Embraced. *Orgasmed* to.

"See you in a bit."

I nodded and laid back on the bed. "Save me some pizza."

When he left, he was still hard and I was still wet, his words hanging thickly in my ear.

"Play with that beautiful pussy and pretend it's his tongue."

God. What had we begun?

17

I sat in the nosebleed section of the conference room, in one of the extra chairs wheeled in from offices and crammed along the wall. If I swiveled too far left or right, my knee hit either Tim Rowland or Charity Freeland, both novice agents with higher sales for the quarter than me. While our office's hierarchy could be easily read by our positions in the room, the giant dry erase board, mounted at one end of the impressive space, also kept score: all sixty-three agents in the company listed and color-coded in order by volume. In green marker and at the top, the rich bitches that always dominated the standings and this conference room. Natalie Bestenbreur. Maria Bott. Jacks Williams. Lorna Pulley, the queen bee herself, currently held court at her standard spot on the northern-most end of the conference table, her gold-tipped Montblanc pen in hand.

"It needs to be trimmed. I don't understand the issue. Get someone out there and do it!" She jabbed the expensive pen into the monogrammed page before her as if it was Neal Blanton's chest.

Neal, our fearless broker who should have retired with his stroke four years ago, sighed. "It's a historical tree. This is downtown, Lorna. You know how these things work. We can't just hack away at it."

I studied the agent list on the whiteboard, drifting down the list, where names went from green ink to black and then, near the bottom, red. I was two names above red, not that getting fired from Blanton & Rutledge would matter in the grand scheme of things. If life grew that dour, I would be submitting resumes for a salaried job anyway, and be out these gilded doors before they had a chance to clean out my desk.

"It's unacceptable." She sniffed, and the skin pulled tight along her ears, an unnatural fold of skin appearing. Her latest facelift had been impressive, but jumped into play at times. I drew a bubble heart in the margin of my agenda to keep from staring.

"You could park in one of the other spots, away from the tree." This brilliant insight was offered by our newest marketing assistant, one of those snarky gays that could insult the last-season pants off you while still winning your affection. His suggestion was laughably ignorant, since the four shaded spots at the forefront of the parking lot were clearly marked.

Sales Person of the Year.
Sales Person of the Month.
Listing Agent of the Year.
Listing Agent of the Month.

It didn't matter if those spots were straddling a landfill, there wasn't an agent with that title who wouldn't tread through fresh shit in order to park there. They'd earned that spot, and Lorna's apple red Bentley was currently parked at an angle between two of them. It was also splattered with bird poo from the family of nine nesting in the branch above her vehicle, which is why we'd wasted the first fifteen minutes of the weekly sales meeting discussing tree trimming and not lead generation, our sales goals, or the broker's open that was occurring in... I snuck a subtle glance at my watch. Four hours.

"If we could move on, Tyler has an excellent presentation on the new FAR-BAR contract that I think we'll all benefit from." Neal swept his good arm toward the thin attorney seated in the middle of the table. Tyler stood, and we all sank a little deeper into our chairs. As unexciting at Lorna's bird shit debacle was, it was still better than a Tyler soliloquy. I carefully switched the cross of my legs and somehow managed to toe Tim in the calf. "Sorry," I mouthed.

"Now, wait a minute." Lorna held up a tan wrist draped in a vintage Cartier watch that, according to office gossip, once belonged to Elton John. "We haven't solved my issue."

"We're going to table the tree trimming conversation until next month," Neal announced with finality and I was disappointed to see Lorna settle back in her seat, her coral-colored lips pinning shut. Lorna and Neal, according to office lore, had a physical tussle in a weekly meeting two decades ago, an event that sadly occurred before the technology of cell phone cameras.

"The new FAR-BAR contract has several changes that will affect buyer's rights." Tyler straightened the lines of his Men's Warehouse suit and wove through the chairs, heading for the 1980's projector at the south end of the room. Our brokerage had closed eight hundred million dollars in real estate last year, yet couldn't invest in a smart TV. He inserted a page under the lamp and cleared his throat. Beside me, I watched Charity open Instagram and scroll through her feed.

Stifling a yawn, I listened to Tyler and sent a grateful prayer up to heaven that I'd never become an attorney. Bored, I ran through the What-Ifs in my life.

What If... Easton hadn't gotten signed by the Marlins? We wouldn't have moved to Miami. He wouldn't have gotten that million-dollar bonus. We wouldn't have bought a four-thousand square foot house that needed six figures worth of work. Would he have proposed so quickly? Would we have stayed in Tallahassee?

What If... I hadn't dropped law school? Would I have learned to love the dry documentation, legal loopholes, and intricate details? Would I still have ended up in real estate, just through a different path?

And the always inevitable What If...

What if I hadn't lost that first baby? What if we'd known that I was pregnant? What if I hadn't gotten so drunk at graduation? What if I had taken vitamins and cut out sodas and—most importantly—not gone to Wakulla Springs and belly-flopped off the high jump? Would the baby have made it safely to birth? Would we have had more? Would I be pushing a stroller right now, instead of listening to this bullshit?

And just as scary... was that still what I wanted? I was beginning to doubt myself, beginning to question whether my fight to be a mother was out of a misplaced need for security and self-worth and not for a life that I actually wanted. We'd started trying for a baby when Easton was in Marlin blue, our bank account fat, my purpose in life fuzzy and unclear. We didn't need my income. I was no longer particularly interested in law. I was a new wife, in love with my husband, and craving something that I couldn't put a finger on. A role. A purpose. Cement that would make our new life and marriage stick.

So we tried for a baby. And when three years of fucking like rabbits didn't work, we brought in the doctors. And when the doctors didn't work, I adopted an adorable baby puppy that grew into a drooling, destructive, and unbehaved mess.

"Let's look at a case study." Tyler replaced the current page with a new one and the energy in the room sank deeper into despair. Beside me, I watched Charity type OMG followed by six emojis on a cat post that wasn't worth a simple like. My own phone hummed against my leg and I carefully pulled it free, giving a casual glance around to make sure no one was watching.

It was an email from the other agent on my pending deal. I reviewed the attachments and sent back a quick response. I was exiting from my email app when I saw an email from Easton that had come through my personal inbox.

Subject Line: Your fantasies...

I'm having trouble concentrating on anything but the things you described.

I scrolled down for more, but there wasn't anything. Just that one indiscernible line.

I knew Easton better than anyone in this world, but couldn't read where he was going with this. If I had to guess, he didn't know himself. I understood that. I had tolerated my fantasies for the last two years because I knew they didn't have potential. They were a photo on a board I could sling darts at, with no actual repercussions, short of some very enjoyable self-induced orgasms. But now they'd—or at least one of those fantasies—had been exposed.

And now he wanted to know if I really wanted it. Why had I shared it with him if I hadn't wanted it to happen? Just to air out my secrets? Or to prompt an action?

Maybe I did want it to happen, I just wanted it to be some magical event that would not affect our lives or relationship in any way at all.

Ha.

My fingers hovered over the screen and I warred over how to respond.

They were just fantasies. We can forget they exist.

I pressed send and let out a contained breath, lifting my head just in time to see Maria Bott's head bob downward, then jerk back upright, her eyes rapidly blinking in an attempt to wake up. Maria's narcoleptic tendencies were why Charity, Tim and I sat at this section of the wall. The timing of her nap would determine which one of us would buy lunch. Prior to the new listings summary: me. Between the start of the listings summary and the end of the meeting: Tim. If she let out an audible snore: Charity.

I moved my phone behind the agenda and did a quick review of the schedule. Tyler's legal update was right before the listings summary. If Maria could hold off this nap for another five or six minutes, I was dining on a steak and cheese sandwich for free.

Tyler flipped to another page and the restlessness in the room grew. I eyed Maria Bott and willed her to keep those big brown eyes flipped open.

My phone hummed, warm against my upper thigh. A response from Easton.

Yeah, we could. Or we could explore them further.

18

"I've never seen so many balls in one place before." Chelsea sucked loudly on a straw, then nudged me with her elbow.

"Yeah, yeah, I got it. Very witty." I pushed my sunglasses on top of my head and squinted at the court, trying to get a better look at this tennis goddess that oozed sexuality. Nicole Fagnani was standing on the right end of the court, her racket in hand, focus on her left Nike. She looked exactly like her internet photos, videos, press interviews, and social media had shown. A normal woman. No one to worry about.

"Here." Chelsea stuck out her binoculars. "I can literally see the wrinkles forming from your squinting."

"Thanks." I used the binoculars and promptly lost the tennis player, three adjustments needed before the tall woman came back into focus.

"How's it going with Aaron?"

I kept the binoculars steady and reminded myself that she was asking an innocent question, with no reason to suspect that Easton and I were fantasizing about adding him to our sex life. "Fine. He talks to Becca a lot. She stopped by the house yesterday."

"Really? Did you talk to her?"

I gave up and handed the pair back to her. "No. I was at work. Easton saw her. She was bitchy to him, and wanted to talk to Aaron alone. The two of them sat out back and fought." That night, Aaron had come back from the gym with a steely expression on his face, one that didn't encourage comment, and went straight to his room. I heard the shower running a few minutes later, and didn't see him the rest of the night. I left a portion of food in the fridge for him, and found the plate rinsed and in the dishwasher the next morning. We'd gone to bed around one, so he'd either been really quiet or eaten really late.

"I can't believe I let her in my mouth." Chelsea unwrapped a stick of gum, then offered me one.

I accepted the piece of Big Red with a smile. "You didn't exactly do her any favors. Cleaning your teeth is like running a marathon with flip flops on. It's possible but exhausting. I doubt she'll miss having you as a client."

"Considering you know next to nothing about dental hygiene *or* running, I'm going to ignore your insult and offer you a juicy piece of gossip in response." Chelsea balled her gum wrapper into a tiny ball and turned to me, the tennis match ignored.

She could have told me that she was transitioning to a panther and it still wouldn't touch the email that—three days later—was still burning a hole through my phone. The email that Easton and I had yet to discuss. The email I saw every time I closed my eyes.

They were just fantasies. We can forget they exist.

— Yeah we could. Or we could explore them further.

It'd been three days and I hadn't had a single impromptu fantasy. Maybe I was cured. Maybe all my body needed was someone to call its bluff.

"You know my dad's neighbor, the guy who leaves his curtains open?"

"Yep." I watched Easton climb up the bleachers toward us, the sun reflecting off his crisp white golf shirt. With khakis, a Rolex, and a pair of tortoiseshell Ray-bans on, he looked every bit the image he wanted to project. Young, cocky, and successful. Would anyone know that two of the four credit cards in his wallet were maxed out?

That the Range Rover we pulled up in had a broken A/C?

That his squeaky-clean wife had tipped the scales in their perfect marriage with her confessions?

"He was arrested this weekend and you'll never guess what for." Chelsea tapped my leg with a nude fingernail, sanded to a point. "Shoplifting."

That was surprising enough for me to pull my attention from Easton, who was almost at our row. "This is the guy in the big house?" On her father's street, every home was enormous. But this guy—if I was thinking of the right guy—was still referred to as the 'big house'. Covering four lots and squatting on an ocean-front piece of real estate that God himself coveted, his house was forty-thousand square feet of ridiculous.

"Yep. And from *Kmart* of all places." She swatted at a fly, then perked up at the sight of a passing woman carrying a blue swab as big as her head. "Oooh, I didn't know they have cotton candy."

Easton arrived at the end of our row and moved sideways, easing past knees, apologizing and flashing that million-dollar smile the entire time. A possessive pit suddenly twisted in my stomach. There was no way Nicole Fagnani wouldn't fall for him. Everyone fell for him. Hell, even Chelsea had had at least six smitten days before she'd seen another shaggy-headed athlete and waltzed away. I glanced back at the court, expecting to see Nicole watching him. Instead, the muscular blonde drilled the tennis ball over the net with a serve that almost cracked the air.

"He was buying microwaves and then returning them, but putting old microwaves in the box." She snorted. "Can you believe that?"

"No, but I'm not sure that's considered shoplifting." I said absently, my eyes catching Easton's as he made it to our seats.

Settling into his, he squeezed my knee. "I miss anything?"

"Yeah, the ball went back and forth over the net," Chelsea remarked. "Oh, and the crowd cheered."

"Thanks. Very helpful." He ran his hand higher up my leg and let it settle on the bare skin just before the hem of my shorts. "I forgot the attention to detail you guys give sports."

"We paid much closer attention to your games," I swore, leaning into him and pressing a kiss on his neck. "And I understood the scoring system, which helped."

"Other than the multiple sexual innuendos I can make about balls, this isn't nearly as exciting," Chelsea drawled. "At least at your games I had asses in baseball pants to stare at."

"I'm so sorry," he quipped. "Next time, I'll pick my clients based on the simplicity of their sports."

"Hey, let's not forget who got you this client," Chelsea pointed out.

"Touché." He lifted his drink and they clinked stadium cups before me. "That's Nic's manager, Anne." He pointed toward the front row, where Shakira was sitting next to a guy that Chelsea swore was Lenny Kravitz, without the dreads. "See the brunette in the hat?"

I saw the brunette. I also noticed the shortening of Nicole's name. Which was an absolutely ridiculous observation given that I was entertaining fantasies and trading emails with my husband about his best friend. And maybe... maybe that was why I was more on edge than possible. Because I wanted to make sure that there was no misunderstanding that my honesty about my proclivities allowed him any sort of leeway at all.

Settling back in his seat, his fingers caressed my thigh in small circles, triggering an instant reaction between my legs. I captured his hand and threaded my fingers through his. He glanced at me. "No deposit yet," he said quietly. "But we set a meeting for Monday. So, hopefully then."

I nodded. "I'm sure she'll do it then." *It* was a transfer of funds, from Morgan Stanley to Easton's firm. Nicole had verbally discussed moving six million dollars over to test the waters—yet had avoided actually pulling the trigger. Easton's one percent management fee on that amount would allow us to pay off the credit cards and cover five months of mortgage payments.

If she followed through.

If *not*, I was wasting a potential open house opportunity by sitting here, and Easton was kissing her athletic ass for nothing. Either way, I needed to swallow my stresses and jealousy and support him through the process. I squeezed his hand and he leaned over, brushing my hair off my neck and planting a gentle kiss just above my pearl necklace. "You are so beautiful."

I turned my head and met his lips, our kiss short and brief, the moment interrupted by Chelsea.

"Hey E." She leaned halfway over my lap and grinned at him. "You know why you should never get into a relationship with a tennis player?"

"Why?"

"Please don't encourage her," I begged, the joke one I was about to hear for the third time.

"Guess." She beamed at him.

"Ummm... they like to smack balls?"

"No, though that is an excellent point." She pushed her sunglasses on the top of her head and paused dramatically. "Because... to them love means nothing."

It was kinda funny, but only because—to Easton and I—love meant everything.

19

My libido woke back up Thursday afternoon, midway through a call with a buyer's agent whose voice sounded like pure sex, dipped in chocolate. I ended the call and pushed away from my desk. Reaching back, I unzipped the top of my skirt, then hitched the Banana Republic number up around my hips. Spinning in the desk chair, I swung the door closed with my toe and flipped the lock. I had a half-hour before Easton got home. Maybe longer, depending on traffic. Plenty of time. I kicked my heels to one side and put my bare feet up on the edge of the desk, opening my knees and working my panties down around my thighs.

I felt edgy. Hungover. The dull headache in the back of my skull throbbed in concert with the ache between my legs. Last night, we'd come home from the charity match drunk, fell asleep without sex, then both overslept. I'd dealt with morning traffic and Wayland's doggie daycare facility, who didn't want to take him after 9am because it would "disrupt the other dogs." Like, what the fuck? He was a hundred-and-forty pounds of unrestrained energy all day long. If he wasn't disrupting the other dogs by his mere presence, something was horribly wrong with him.

I was knuckle deep, my ass digging into the seat, my fantasies deep into a role-play where a commission shortage could only be solved by my mouth, when our front door slammed shut.

I paused, my sexual thoughts fleeing to the open vent in my floor, where they ran off to die. Footsteps sounded and I tried to place their location in the house. Working my panties back into place, I yanked a tissue out from the holder and wiped off my fingers. Zipping up the back of my skirt, I quietly disengaged the lock and crept out of the office. The person had gone into the formal living room, then the den, best I could tell from the acoustics.

I took the opposite path, rounded the corner into the kitchen, and screamed. My toe caught painfully on the transom, and I grabbed the frame to keep from falling. "Aaron!"

He looked over from his place at the fridge, a can of Mountain Dew in hand. One eyebrow lifted in a bemused fashion. "Elle. You okay?"

"Are you the only one here?"

"Yep. Just came in. I thought you were sleeping."

"No, I was in the office." I pointed an unnecessary finger in the general direction of the office. "Prepping a listing agreement. A bungalow in Meadow Hills. You know that neighborhood? It's really nice. They aren't craftsman-style, they're like Tudor. Mid-century modern Tudor."

He squinted at me. "Did you take an Adderall?"

So, I was talking too much. I crossed my arms over my chest and did my best to amble toward the sink in as casual a manner as possible, well aware that my panties were still stuck to me from my recent activities. "Nah. I might have overdone it on expresso. I'm still catching up from last night." I clamped my mouth shut before I said anything else.

He closed the fridge and turned to the island, setting a Pyrex container of sliced watermelon on the granite. "Want some?"

"Sure." I glanced at the microwave clock. "What are you doing here? I thought you'd be on-site somewhere."

"I've got a meeting with Becca and the counselor at four. Wanted to get a shower first, clean up a little."

Yeah. My gaze trailed over his shirt, which was stuck to his strong shoulders and chest. There was a dusting of sawdust over his arms and back, the smell of it and grass drifting off of him. I took a step back and reconsidered my need for watermelon, well aware of the still-wet condition of my lady parts. Moving to the cabinet, I opened the door and reached for a glass. "How's counseling going?"

They'd had two appointments so far, and I hadn't spoken to him after either. I'd asked Easton for an update, but had gotten a shrug in response. I shut the cabinet door.

"It's been a gigantic waste of money so far." He plucked a cube of watermelon from the tray and popped it into his mouth. "She's refusing to give me a reason why she started hooking up with him. She says she needs to learn who she is, which I guess she plans to do in his bed. She's at his house right now. Is probably fucking him before our session." His face hardened into stern lines.

"And the divorce is definitely happening?" I still couldn't fathom it. My marriage was the only solid thing in my life. Our relationship was my bedrock. My heartbeat. I couldn't understand Becca jumping ship and not looking back.

"Yep. Today is the last court-ordered counseling session. We've sorted out the house and the business through mediation, so we just have to get through today, then have an attorney review the agreement and then..." He drew his thumb across the front of his throat. "It's final."

"That quickly? It's been..." I tried to do the math. "Three weeks? Two and a half?"

"The beauty of living in Florida. The thirty-day divorce. As long as we agree on the division of assets, then it's quick and simple." He shrugged. "The shitty part is that we've spent more time arguing over the house than discussing our relationship." *A house he ended up giving to her in exchange for her half of his business.* "And it'd be less painful if she was leaving me for a good guy, but he's a *complete* dick." He grimaced, the hurt clear across his features.

Yeah. That was one thing that Easton had described in clarity—Aaron's introduction to the guy, who had been waiting outside their first mediation session, his chest puffed, arm slung around Becca's shoulder as if marking her as his territory. My heart had broken at the way he'd been treated, and I'd mentally ignited any remaining compassion for Becca.

"I'm so sorry." I felt a stab of guilt for avoiding him these last few days. "You don't deserve any of this."

"No, but I'm almost glad it happened." He set down the watermelon and reached for his Mountain Dew. "What if we'd had kids together? What if I hadn't found out about it until it was too late?"

"Yeah."

"You've been busy lately." He pulled the tab of the soda can and looked at me. "I've barely seen you around."

"Yeah. Work has been crazy." I could feel the blush hit my cheeks, and wondered if my absence had been that transparent. Ever since the awkwardness after Vegas, I had scheduled everything around avoiding Aaron, an effort that had also significantly cut into my time with Easton. Something had to change, and maybe this conversation would break the awkwardness and move us back onto casual footing.

"I'd hoped it wasn't because of me." His gaze dropped to the kitchen floor. "And what happened in Vegas."

Oh my God. He was actually bringing this up right now, right here, with nowhere for me to escape and nothing to distract us from the conversation. So much for turning things around.

I clutched the empty glass and forced myself to walk to the sink and reach for the nozzle. "No, it wasn't that."

"But Easton told you, right?"

"Yeah." I turned on the water and watched as it filled the glass.

"I just didn't want things to be weird. Especially since he'd offered for me to stay here. But it is, isn't it?"

I turned off the water. "No, it's fine."

"Elle." My name was a rope, one that snagged my chin and pulled it toward him. He rested his weight on the counter and met my eyes. "I'm fucked up right now. I'm in a really weird place, and you two are my best friends. I was drunk and I was horny and I fucked up. Please forgive me. I can't—" he swallowed. "I don't want to do anything that's going to mess up things between you two, or with us."

"It's not..." I sighed, my heart breaking at the desperate way he looked at me. There was such fear in his eyes, so much vulnerability in each line of his body, despite his strong stance. "You didn't do anything wrong." I wet my lips and continued. "I knew you were there. I saw you on the balcony and I told Easton that. Not right then, but afterward, like you did. I could have stopped him and I didn't. So don't feel guilty. It wasn't just you. I was drunk too. We all were." I took a long sip of the water, then set it down. "And I've been weird because I didn't know how you felt about it, and I didn't want you to think any differently of me. But—I'll stop avoiding you."

"I'd never think differently of you. Please tell me you know that."

It was a genuinely nice sentiment, but I'd been on the judgment end of things too many times to believe it. "Look, I want to be there for you, and I haven't. And I'm sorry I haven't supported you through this. I mean, E..." I let out a strangled laugh. "E gives shit relationship advice. He once told Chelsea to send a thank you letter after a date."

He laughed, and there was a well-needed break in the tension, a tilt of the axis back to normal. "Yeah, he does give shit advice."

"Just do the opposite of whatever he suggests," I grinned.

"Here, I'll get you some ice." He held out his hand and I passed him the glass.

"Thanks."

"Don't beat yourself up about Becca." He spoke over his shoulder as he pulled out an ice tray and twisted the plastic, breaking up the cubes. "Honestly, it's been a financial and legal headache, but emotionally?" He shrugged. "Other than a massive hit to my ego, I'm okay. I'm almost relieved. For a year now, I've felt this wall between us, and I haven't been able to figure out how to knock it down. It's been kind of nice to have a break and just say fuck it."

"Yeah, I guess. But it's scary. I remember how much you loved her on your wedding day."

He wiped his palm on his pants, then carefully picked out a few chunks of ice, dropping them into my glass. "The rough part is, a large part of me still does. You spend four years of your life with someone, and they have a piece of it. I didn't stop loving her the day I found out. I just started hating her at the same time."

I could understand that. But I also didn't feel—wasn't sure—that *she* still loved *him*. I couldn't imagine someone falling in love with a new person if they were still in love with their husband, and couldn't justify her treating Aaron the way she was if she loved him at all.

"So, anyway, I need you to find me a girl. Someone filthy in bed and uninterested in emotional attachment." He extended the glass of water with a grin. "And apparently *not* a famous tennis star."

"Ha." I pulled out the stool that hid under the island and climbed onto it. "Easton told you about last night?"

After the tennis event, we'd had drinks with Nicole who was incredibly delightful, bless my jealousy's soul, and incredibly gay. Like... super gay. As a prime example, my neck *may* contain a hickey from my husband's new client's Olympic-gold mouth—the result of a tequila shot taken a little too far. He was right. Nicole did reek of sexuality. Sexuality that really really liked me and not my husband. Not that Easton had minded. I'd seen the gleam in his eyes as she had gotten more and more handsy. He'd given me a suggestive grin and I'd vigorously shook my head at him, killing the idea of a Nicole/Aaron/Elle sandwich.

"You're preening," Aaron remarked.

"Am I?" I blushed and bit into a wedge of melon. To be honest, the attention had been nice.

"I'm actually surprised you're functioning properly. E said you'd had a half-dozen drinks." He gave me the sort brotherly look that Easton liked to adopt, right before he reminded me to wear my seat belt, or not give rides to homeless people, or to call him when I got into an Uber.

"I did, and I was fine." I waved off his concern. "I handle my alcohol way better than you think."

"In Vegas, you vomited in the ice bucket of the limo," he reminded me.

"I did?" I frowned at him, and the faint memory of clutching the ice bucket did sharpen into focus. "No, I didn't. You have me confused with one of those escorts. I was sober and classy the entire time."

He smirked at me, and I wondered if he was thinking about watching me through the window.

"Almost the entire time," I amended. "Definitely no vomiting occurred."

He chewed on another chunk of watermelon and let my lie slide. "So, Nicole's gay."

"Very." I shrugged. "But you never know. Maybe she'd cross the street for you."

"Nah." He tore off a piece of paper towel and used it to wipe the watermelon juice off his fingers. "I watched an interview she did with 30-for-30 and she didn't do anything for me anyway. I prefer brunettes." He grinned at me, and I couldn't help but return the gesture. He'd always been a flirt, and this easy back and forth returned us to familiar ground.

"Here." He pushed the watermelon container toward me. "I'm going to go take a shower and clean up so my future ex-wife can throw a bunch of bullshit on me." He pointed at me. "Drink lots of water."

I rolled my eyes in response. "Don't leave your wet towel on the floor."

"Come on." He scoffed, spreading his hands as he walked. "Who do you think you're talking to?"

"Uh-huh." I pulled the container closer to me and selected a bigger piece. "Go tell someone who will believe you."

I heard him laugh as he walked down the hall and let out a slow breath of relief, glad that things were back to normal between us. Picking up my glass, I stared into the clear contents. God, I *had* thrown up in that limo. How had I forgotten that? I tilted back my head and finished off the glass, shaking the ice until a piece landed into my mouth.

There was the sound of the front door and I turned, watching as Wayland's nose wedged through the opening. He barreled through, my husband in tow.

20

Two days later, I was mid-huff up the highest part of our street when Easton pulled Wayland's leash over his wrist and tossed out the grenade.

"You never responded to my email."

The email was now a solid week old, which I'd hoped had been long enough to fall off our radar.

They were just fantasies. We can forget they exist.

Yeah, we could. Or we could explore them further.

"It didn't require a response," I pointed out.

"Yeah, but it probably should have." We hit the top part of the hill and moved to the shoulder to let a white SUV past. "Have you thought about it anymore?"

"Thought about what?" *Which part? Who?*

"Any of it." We paused to let Wayland take a long and very intense examination of an untamed clump of grass. "Have you thought about Aaron at all?"

"He lives with us. It's hard not to think about someone when you're tripping over them." I was evading and he knew it. The next step would be a confrontation, one paired with his serious voice and some eye contact.

"Elle." He moved in front of me and blocked my path, his gaze searing a hole in my eyes. "I'm trying to make you happy."

I pulled at the two plastic grocery bags I'd tucked into the front of my shorts and nodded at Wayland. "Your son is pooping." I moved toward the Great Dane and E blocked me.

"Elle."

"Easton."

"Talk to me."

"Okay. I don't want to do anything with Aaron."

"Why?"

I blew out a frustrated breath. "Because it'll make things really really awkward."

"I thought you guys talked and were back to normal."

I frowned at him. "Where did you get that?"

He suddenly became aware of the giant pile that Wayland had created. Passing me the leash, he took the bags and doubled them up. "It just seems like you're good again."

"Bullshit." I followed him, tugging on Wayland's leash to keep him out of the street, and pulverized a daisy head in my distracted journey. "Did you talk to him?"

"I talk to him all the time. He mentioned you spoke. Nothing to freak out about."

"I don't like you guys talking about me. Especially not with all of..." My blood chilled. "You didn't tell him about the other night, right? The role-play thingy we did?"

"No." Easton squatted beside the pile and carefully worked it into the bag, somehow staying spotless through the process. "But—"

I waited.

He brushed the back of his forearm across his forehead, then jerked the bag handles up and tied them in a note.

"But what?"

"He felt like shit about the whole voyeurism thing, so I told him not to worry about it. I told him you liked it." The final sentence was softer than the first, tossed over his shoulder as if it was superstitious salt, and then run from—his long legs clipping toward the trash can at the end of the driveway.

I stood in place, my hands crossed over my chest, and waited for him to return, doing an emergency sweep of the street for anything big and brutal enough to kill him with. Unless I was going to rip a mailbox out of the ground bare-handed, I was out of luck. When he came back, his gaze studiously locked on Wayland, I spoke. "You told him *I liked it*? Are you out of your fucking mind?"

"What? You did like it!" His attention cut to me and carried a flash of the careless attitude that typically drenched my panties.

"And sometimes you like to fuck me in schoolgirl outfits, but I don't run down and tell the local fucking nuns," I countered. "I can't—I won't—be honest with you if I can't trust you. That wasn't your information to tell, it was mine."

"But you wouldn't have told him."

I sputtered. "I didn't need to tell him! Why the fuck would I tell him?!"

"To see how he reacted." Something came over his face then, a knowing cocky grin that made me want to slap him across the cheek and then straddle the resulting mark. He had something. A card up his sleeve. Something that tilted this playing field.

"And?" I couldn't help it. I literally *couldn't* contain the word.

He shrugged. "I shouldn't be talking about it. As you just pointed out, this isn't my stuff to tell. If you want to know, talk to Aaron."

I tackled him in his backward step, my leg hooking around his knee at the same time that I collided with his shoulders. He went down, Wayland lunged for us, and I landed a solid punch to his solar plexus before Wayland was on top of me, his nails digging into my left thigh, his back beginning to curve as he started doing the worst possible thing, short of me getting into a physical altercation in the middle of our hoity-toity neighborhood.

He started to hump me.

"Wayland!" I shrieked, hitting his chest with my hand. "Get off! Down!" I found the cord of his leash and yanked. He started to pant. My husband, who had worked his way up to his elbows, one hand pressed against the center of his abdomen, started to laugh. I rolled right, and was almost on top of the poop spot when I realized my error and went left. Wayland scrambled to follow, and I screamed as one of his paws pistoned into my cheek.

"Wayland," Easton spoke in the calm voice of someone who wasn't inches from excrement-smeared grass. "Stop." He found the end of the leash and pulled, dragging Wayland off of me.

I took a deep breath and sat up, dusting off the dirt from his paws. My knit top was, without a doubt, ruined. "Stop playing games with me and just tell me exactly what your conversation with Aaron was."

He crouched and held out his hand, helping me to my feet. "I told him to stop worrying about it. That you had a bit of a voyeuristic streak and that it had turned you on."

I dug my nails into the back of his hands as I pulled upright. "And?"

"And he said..." he took a moment to place the right words. "He said "interesting"."

"That was the big smirk you gave me? Because he said *interesting?*"

"Look, I really don't want to rehash our entire conversation. It was personal shit. All you need to know is that he's absolutely fine with you being fine with him seeing us." He grinned at me.

"Uh-uh. No. I need you to rehash the entire conversation, especially considering that it was about me."

"He thought it was hot. He thinks you're the sexiest woman in Miami. He, in an absolutely respectful way"—he held up his hands as if to ward off another attack—"told me that I was lucky as hell and to never let you go. That's it. End of conversation."

"You are lucky," I pointed out grudgingly. "Exceedingly so."

"Exceedingly so," he allowed. "And..." he looped a finger in the waist of my shorts and pulled me closer. "I do have the sexiest woman in the world. Which is why I'm trying to keep you happy in the bedroom."

"I'm very happy in the bedroom." I took the kiss he gave, then pulled back. "But don't talk to Aaron about me anymore." It was hard not to feel a sticky warmth at what Aaron had said. Sexiest woman in Miami? He'd thought our sex was hot?

There was a boost that occurred when Easton gave me compliments, an effect that had slowly diminished over time. At one point, I would have glowed over him telling me I was beautiful. Now, I felt a minor satisfaction over a met obligation—and not much more. But this new stimulus... it brought back that old feeling, that buzz of fresh excitement and nervousness. It wasn't just that Aaron thought I was sexy, it was Easton's reaction. He loved that his best friend found me hot. I could see it in his cocky grin, could feel the energy in his touch.

I stepped back from Easton as if it would physically separate me from the sensation.

"I won't." He tilted his head toward the bottom of the hill. "Ready to head back? I promise not to bring up orgies over dinner if you make macaroni and cheese."

"Ugh." I dropped my arms and trudged in the direction of home. "We don't have noodles. Fish tacos?"

"Deal." He dropped a kiss on my head and switched Wayland's leash so he could hold my hand.

21

The divorce became final on Tuesday, the same day as my ill-fated but barely successful closing. Easton and I were in the midst of an argument on whether to get Wayland his own Whopper Jr when I got the text from Chelsea, who heard the news from Becca's sister.

I glanced at my phone, cut Easton off mid-sentence, and told him the news. Abandoning our spot in the Burger King drive-through, we cut across the parking lot, hopped a curb, and headed for home. From the backseat, Wayland let out a mournful whine.

"I told you, he knows." Easton tried to reach back and pet his head, but Wayland slunk to the passenger side, out of reach.

"It doesn't matter if he knows. He doesn't have to get something just because we are getting something. That expectation teaches him to beg."

"Not getting him something teaches him to beg. You don't know that, because you never get him anything, and he always begs."

"Did Aaron text you? I can't believe that Chelsea found this out before we did. Take Freeman over. Madison Ave is going to be ridiculous."

"I haven't heard anything from him."

"Maybe he's at the house."

He was at the house. I stopped in the kitchen and spied him sitting on the back deck, one flip-flopped foot propped up on our hibiscus pot. As I watched, he twisted the cap off of his beer and tossed it in the general direction of the trash can. Easton came beside me and followed my gaze through the window.

"Look," I whispered, pointing to the papers on the patio table beside Aaron. It was a thick stack, gem-clipped together at the top, with a court seal pressed into the cover page. "Chelsea was right. The divorce is done."

"Poor guy."

"He's just staring at the pool."

"He's probably wondering why we can't afford to fix it."

"Or why we haven't stuck some koi out there." Our pool had been at the top of a renovation list we'd never begun, the broken pump and cracked walls now framing a three-foot pond of algae-thick sludge that occupied the deep end and rose and fell with the rain levels.

"I think you'd have to install an air filter or pump, in order for koi to live."

"She's such a bitch. I can't believe we introduced them. Technically, this is partly our fault. You think he's crying?"

"He's not a big cryer. Remember when we watched *Armageddon*?"

"Not everyone cries in that movie. I think he cried at their wedding. When she was walking down the aisle?"

"Those could have been tears of remorse."

"Or allergies."

"Or your onion breath." I gripped his arm. "Wait, something's happening." Aaron's head turned slowly to one side, his strong profile visible.

"Elle?" Aaron said my name clearly, at a normal volume, and I stiffened.

"Yes?"

"You know, the doggie door is open. I can hear everything you guys are saying."

Easton glared at me and I shot the look right back at him. "I didn't open it!" I whispered.

"You should have checked," he hissed.

"Yeah, I can hear that too. The acoustics out here are incredible. It's like being in a concrete bowl."

At least he didn't sound like he was crying. I pushed by Easton and pulled open the door, giving him a cautious smile. "Hey there."

"God, you guys have convoluted conversations. Your concern for me was overshadowed by like nine other things."

"We were getting back around to you," Easton said, following me out onto the porch and pulling the door shut behind him.

"Well, I'm fine." Aaron took a sip of the beer, his gaze returning to the pool.

"You don't have to be fine," I moved the other chair into the shaded part of the porch and sat in it. "It's okay to be upset."

"Honestly, I'm just exhausted right now. I'm just glad it's over. C'est la vie."

I watched as he took another sip of beer, his handsome features blank and unemotional. He did look exhausted. I thought of him in the limo, the way he'd closed his eyes and rested his head back on the seat. What had he said? That he was tired. *Tired and heartbroken.*

Three and a half weeks later, and he certainly hadn't gotten any rest.

Easton picked up the stack of papers. "This looks thick."

"That's what she said." He gave a weak smile, then lifted his shoulders in a shrug. "It's all legal jargon. I didn't even read it. If she's fucking me, she's fucking me."

Easton shot me a look and I subtly shook my head, not wanting him to push Aaron, especially when he was in this mood.

I pushed out of the chair and opened the cooler. Shifting

through the half-melted ice, I snagged two more beers. Cracking the tops off both, I passed one to E. "Hey. To new beginnings."

Aaron held out his beer. "To new beginnings."

We clinked bottles and I saw a bit of the tension ease out of Aaron's shoulders.

We finished a case of Bud Light over fish tacos, all while sharing every terrible story we had about Becca. I told them about the time she borrowed my Betsy Johnson purse which had twenty dollars in the inside pocket, and returned it sans the cash. Aaron told us about the time she got so drunk that she told his Cuban grand-mother that political refugees were the downfall of the South Florida economy and culture. We were horrible and cruel and laughed harder as the night grew later. At ten-thirty, I sent her a text that outlined in typo-riddled clarity, all the reasons that she was a terrible person. At eleven-fifteen, we decided to Viking funeral the copy of the divorce papers and spent thirty drunk minutes assembling a boat. Easton produced a cracked skimboard as a base, and we created a structure out of beer bottles, a starter log and twigs, the stack of papers set on top and then doused in Wild Turkey.

Sitting on the top step of the pool, I watched as Aaron stood in the dry shallow end and held a lighter over the bottom of the pile. Flames flickered and he carefully pushed the board forward, the mini-island cutting a path through the green water of the deep end. A few feet in, it ignited.

I cheered and the boys joined in, Easton tilting back his head and letting out a long howl that brought Wayland barreling into the picture, his own head lifting to join in. I tried to mimic the sound, my tiny voice soon paired with Aaron's, the sounds lifting into the night sky along with the crackle and smoke of Aaron's marriage.

22

The Range Rover's air conditioning was still out, so Easton and I took my car to dinner. Friday nights in Miami used to mean Smith & Wollensky's, but our new budget constraints now meant we crossed 395 and went to a mom and pop steakhouse that felt upscale if you got drunk early and didn't mind stained linen napkins.

I gave my car keys and a kiss to Easton when he walked in the house, a bottle of cheap Moscato already half gone, my skin buzzing. I'd written a contract on an eighteen-month rental—oceanfront—that would bring in four thousand dollars, and I wanted to celebrate. I'd already bought a new pair of shoes, a slightly too-small but on sale pair of Jimmy Choos that would make a Catholic priest reconsider his vows. My pinky toes were already burning in pain. When we walked up the cobblestoned path to the restaurant's front door, I swallowed a wince at the rub of pink leather against toe.

"You okay?" Easton pulled open the door and frowned at me, his gaze dropping to my feet.

"Perfect," I said breezily, sweeping by him and into the restaurant. A bored teenager stood behind the front desk and gave me a slack look. "Reservation for two," I managed. "It's under North."

He didn't even look at the board. "K. Follow me."

I followed him and thought about my first job, also as a restaurant hostess, and what my manager would have done if I had said "K" in response to a customer's statement. Diane Rutledge had been a screamer. I would have been yanked into the kitchen, dressed down in front of the cooking staff, then tossed back into the restaurant with orders to wrap silverware until my hands were numb.

The kid did, at least, pull out my chair. I sank into it with a pleased sigh.

"Long day?" Easton asked.

"Good day." I unrolled the silverware and put the napkin across my lap. "You?"

"Slow. No money from Nicole yet. I met with a Heats player, but I don't think anything is going to happen there. He's meeting with David Sax on Monday."

David Sax. The kiss of death and ball-sucker of all athletes. Not literally, but we liked to say it when he stole a client from Easton. It helped ease the pain of the fact that Sax was likely clueless Easton even existed.

"I'm surprised Nicole hasn't moved anything over yet. Have you talked to her?" I heard the nagging side of me kick into gear, the side that wanted to drill him on thinking positively, following up with his prospects via email, and working his center of influence. I confronted that side and forced her down my throat. No more questions, I promised myself. Just enjoy yourself.

"I've spoken with her every day since the tennis event. She's non-committal." He sighed. "I feel like I'm a vulture, but at the same time, I don't have the energy to listen to her talk about her day when all I really need to know is if she's wasting my fucking time."

"Every day?" I frowned. "For how long?"

"Ten, fifteen minutes."

"E, that's way too much contact for her not have pulled the trigger."

"I know. But I need that deposit. I haven't brought in a new client since March."

A fact I was painfully aware of. I closed my menu and pushed it to the side. "She's a big girl. Be upfront and ask her when she is going to move over some of her funds." So much for swallowing the nag.

"I *have* asked her." He scowled and I could feel the turn of the conversation hovering in the half-empty room. "She won't give me a straight answer."

"Maybe you could bring her a specific investment opportunity." Okay, there. That was it. I would shut my mouth after that one. I mentally locked my lips up and threw away the key.

He met my eyes and the corner of his mouth crooked up. "Okay. Any other advice?"

"You should wear that shirt more. You look delicious in it."

"You should take that dress off. It's covering up all of your best parts." He grinned.

"I'm not sure the restaurant would be okay with that."

The restaurant picked that moment to interrupt, a lanky waiter approaching with a crooked bowtie and the same dull expression that the host had carried. Maybe they all got high together just before work. I listened politely as he rattled through a list of specials, then ordered the same thing I always got—the steak medallions, medium rare, dry baked potato on the side.

Easton ordered the yellowtail fettuccine, then passed back his menu and gave me a wry grin. "Remember post-game dinners?"

Of course I did. He would get the bone-in filet topped with lobster. We'd pick through a smorgasbord of appetizers while sipping wine flights. Dessert was an afterthought but paired with a sweet wine or spiked coffee, our long meal tended to by three attentive waiters who were rewarded handsomely with an eye-popping tip.

We had lived large and recklessly and had absolutely nothing to show for it but blurred, half-drunk memories. I took a sip of water and pretended it was wine. "I miss the lobster."

"I'll catch some for you," he promised. "We'll drive down to Marathon for mini-season."

We wouldn't, but I still smiled at the thought. Maybe we would. Maybe there'd be a cheap hotel rate online, and we'd actually find our fins and we'd dive and net lobsters and feast like kings.

"You know what I miss?" He settled back in his chair and played with the setting of his silverware. "Guthrie's nights."

"Aw." I propped an elbow on the table and rested my chin on the pad of my hand. "Me too. God, I'd kill for a Gut-box right now." The greasy fried chicken fingers, paired with crinkle fries and an ice-cold coke... there hadn't been a better meal in Tallahassee at 3am.

"Remember our list?"

"Of course. I still have it somewhere. I remember reading it on our wedding day." I had kept the smudged page, folded into quarters, Easton's cramped handwriting in neat rows down the page.

Elle & Easton's List of Happy Things

It had been a long list, divided into past, present and future. Our past items included Chelsea's vomit at Potbelly's, Safety Not Guaranteed, doggie-style (which we had originally deemed as our favorite position), Cherry Slushies, and our first kiss.

Our present items had included Gut Boxes, Seminoles Baseball, the way he studied my mouth before kissing me, microwave s'mores—which I argued should go on the future list as well, but he said we may get tired of them. "I told you we'd never get tired of microwave s'mores," I pointed out. "And look, I was right."

"You were right." He smiled, that slow and warm smile that

seemed as if it was made for me. "How could I have been so stupid?"

"Well, you had a good response." I tilted my head to one side, remembering it. "I told you that everything in life paled compared to microwave s'mores, and you told me that everything in life paled compared to me."

"And then I proposed." His eyes crinkled at the edges.

"And then you proposed," I said softly. "And I said yes."

"What were you thinking?"

I laughed. "What were you? You weren't even able to get down on one knee. And you wouldn't have wanted to, not in that disgusting lot."

"And I didn't have a ring."

"Total impulse."

"It was the best decision I ever made in my life." He leaned forward and captured my hand, running his thumb over the back of it. "I wouldn't change it, Guthrie's parking lot and all."

I wouldn't either. I loved the memory of that night, the excitement I'd had at the idea of being Mrs. Easton North for the rest of my life. I had pushed the to-go container onto the floorboard and crawled across the center console and gotten into his lap. He'd smelled like baseball leather, sweat and chicken and tasted like root beer and French fries. We'd called my mom and then his, waking them both up with the news.

"What was on our future list? A World Series ring." He grimaced.

"A baby," I said quietly.

His hand tightened on mine. "What else?"

"A house big enough for our family." I almost said our kids. Five kids. That's what we'd written down on the list. We'd argued over that too. I'd wanted three and he'd wanted six. Somehow, we'd agreed on five, but I'd written "or three" in small parentheses after the number, followed by a smiley face. Everything was smiley faces and hearts back then.

"We got the house and the dog."

"I don't think a dog was on the list." And the house I'd had in mind hadn't been the sprawling fixer-upper we'd ended up with.

"Law school." I made my own face.

"Do you ever still think about that?" He let go of my hand and crossed his arms on top of the table, his elbows almost too wide for the round top.

"No." I shook my head. "Honestly, I don't. I meant it when I quit." I'd dropped the program six weeks in, right around the time he'd started playing. He'd pushed against it, worried that I was forgoing my dream for his, but I'd stood my ground then, and I reemphasized that now. "I don't want to be an attorney."

"And you're happy in real estate?"

"I'm..." I drew a line down the condensation on the outside of my glass. "I think I'll like real estate more when I start selling more. Right now, it's very stressful, because each deal feels like it's crucial."

"Yeah. I'm right there with you." He looked away as the waiter set down our plates, then waited for him to leave before continuing. "This is temporary, the struggle. Your business is growing, so is mine. We'll get through this."

"I know." My grin widened. "Even when it sucks, there's no one I'd rather be beside. I love our life together."

"Yeah?" He studied me. "Because you deserve so much more."

I frowned. "I deserve you. I'm exactly where I should be. So are you."

"God, you're too good for me." He said it so sincerely, as if it didn't matter that the major part of our future list—a family—was missing. And maybe it didn't matter. Maybe we would find a new list.

And maybe, just like I didn't need his success—he didn't need my babies.

He picked up his fork. "Let's eat. I have somewhere I want to take you after dinner."

After dinner took us to a dark parking lot in Doral, close enough to MIA that I could feel the planes taking off. I rolled down the window and stared at the neon sign. "A strip club?" I'd been thinking Ben & Jerry's. Possibly a veer-off at the Redbox at Tropicaire. Maybe, for old time's sake, a cherry Slushy.

"It's not a strip club. It's a couples club."

I looked back at the building, which sat across from an extended stay hotel and shared a strip mall with a tile store. "A couples club."

"I created an online profile and everything. It seems legit. You have to pay a membership fee in order to attend. They have rooms that you can have sex in while people watch."

I stared at my husband who had to have lost his mind. "*What?* I'm not going in there."

He tilted his head at me. "I thought you liked that. Like with Aaron."

"I—" I took a moment to collect myself and tried to work through the complex web of reasons why what had happened in Vegas was completely different than this strip mall with a bunch of random strangers. "This—this does not turn me on."

"Let me pull up their site and show you the pics."

"E." I put my hand over his phone. "Stop. I appreciate you doing this, but please stop. This doesn't do anything for me." *This would never do anything for me.*

There was an audible click as he locked his phone. "Fine. Okay. Sorry." He reached back and pulled at his seatbelt, then fastened it into the latch.

I looked out the window and watched a plane come in, my BMW's seat vibrating from the turbulence. "I wish I could explain it to you. It's just... different."

He pulled out of the lot and accelerated hard through the turn.

For the fourteen minutes it took to get home, we rode in silence and I regretted every single thing I had told him.

23

We undressed in stony silence, each sound magnified. The clunk of his watch as it hit the dresser. The scrape of the hanger against the rod. I pulled off my dress shorts and tossed them toward the hamper, falling short of the basket. He sat on the edge of the bed, toed off his boots and left them where they fell. Wayland slunk under the bed and hid, his tail sticking out.

"I'm going to take a shower."

"Sure." He didn't look at me. I was pulling the bathroom door shut when he spoke. "Wait."

I waited. I would always, forever, wait if he asked me to.

"Come here." He reached out his hand. I came, and he gathered me against him, his arms around my thighs, his face buried against my stomach. I ran my fingers through his hair and he looked up at me. "I'm sorry."

"You don't have to be sorry. You were trying to do something for me and I reacted poorly to it."

"I'm lost, Elle. You won't tell me what turns you on, so I'm guessing over here. You won't let me talk to Aaron, and won't tell me who else turns you on. You don't want a stranger from a club, so who? Who do you want?"

"You. You turn me on. I don't need anyone else."

"Yeah, well. You also say you don't need a baby. And I can't give you that. Or..." he threw a hand in the general direction of the rest of our house. "Or fix up this house. *Fuck*, Elle." He pushed me a step back and stood. "I can't give you anything. But I can give you this."

I looked at him, horrified. "I don't want you to do anything because of—"

"It's not just that." He rested his hands on his hips and stared at the floor. "It's also because it turns me the fuck on to see you in your sexual element. It makes me feel this raw need to hold you down and fuck a dozen orgasms out of you. And thinking about watching another man have you—it shouldn't turn me on but it does. Fuck, it does. I hate it but now it's in my head and I don't know what to do with it."

I wanted to believe what he was saying. I wanted to embrace my feelings with the belief that we were turned on by the same things, but everything he just said terrified me.

Was this what he wanted? Or was he just trying to—in one aspect of our lives—give me what he felt I deserved?

I reached for him and slid my hands up the pinstripes on his dress shirt, then gripped it at his collar. "I don't know that you'd feel that way if it actually happened. I don't know if I would feel the same way. It's too risky. We can't undo something like that. You won't be able to erase the image of me with another man. You told me that you'd kill another man who touched me. That the thought made you crazy, even though it turned you on. What's changed since then?"

It was a vomit of every fear I had. I spewed it all out, and then desperately wanted to take it back.

"I don't know," he admitted. "It still makes my blood boil, but it's like that anger, that masculine fury—like it makes the thought even hotter. The more I've been thinking about it, the more I can't stop thinking about it."

"What if you're wrong and it taints everything?"

His eyebrows knitted in thought. "So it's not the act that you're afraid of. It's the consequences?"

I paused, considering the question. "I guess. Though—that club —that wasn't about consequences. The idea of that freaked me out. I…" I swallowed, trying to find the right words for the emotions that had churned on our car ride home. "I didn't feel like I would be in control in there. And I don't mean that I want to be dominant—I just need to know that we only do things that I feel comfortable with. I want to feel safe. Cherished. Worshipped." I blushed at the bare confession. "And there, I wouldn't feel any of that. I don't care what was inside that door. It freaked me out."

I saw the moment he got it, his face falling with understanding and regret. He waited for me to finish, then cradled me into his chest, pressing a kiss to the top of my head. "You're right. Completely. I feel like a fucking idiot."

"Don't, I—"

He shushed me. "Elle. I was an idiot. But I also needed to know everything you just told me. I can't read your mind."

I nodded against his chest. "Okay." I gave him a squeeze, then stepped back and turned. "Get my zipper?"

He gathered my hair to one side and carefully tugged on the zipper. "What if we start with something small?"

I waited as he dragged it down.

"Someone watching, but with just you and I together. And during it—if you want more, then you can instigate that." His knuckles brushed against my shoulder blades as he unclipped my bra. "But it will be the Elle show. Everything focused on your pleasure, and somewhere you feel safe." His hands slid around to the front and cupped my breasts under the loose bra.

I smiled and rotated to face him, peeling off the shirt. "If you want to cop a feel, you can just ask."

"I'm asking." There was still a wariness in his eyes and I grabbed his hands and placed them on my breasts in an attempt to chase the hesitancy away.

Raising on my toes, I put my mouth at his ear. "I think I like that idea."

"Yeah?" His hands tightened, his thumbs brushing tenderly over my nipples. "Because that turns me the fuck on." He leaned down and kissed my neck. "You need these panties anymore?"

I reached down before he had the chance to rip them off and skimmed them off. "Better?"

"Better. Touch me."

I undid his belt and his jeans and let out a happy sigh as my hand closed around his cock. He hadn't lied. My husband was turned on, stiff to the point of steel. I flicked my gaze up to meet his eyes, and any hesitancy was gone from their depths.

He grinned, a wickedly delicious expression of pure confidence and promise. My own smile widened and I gripped him tighter, anxious for what was about to come.

"On your knees," he ordered. "And open up your throat."

24

An hour later, I was flat on my back in the middle of the mattress beside Easton. Wayland was sprawled on his back in the middle of his pad, snoring loudly. On the TV, a Big Bang rerun involving Billy Bob Thornton played, the volume almost too low to hear.

"You think you could actually do it? Have sex while someone watches?"

I turned my face toward Easton. "Uh—yeah. I've already done that."

"But you were drunk," he pointed out. "And you had plausible deniability that you were aware of it. It might be different when it's arranged."

"Maybe," I conceded. "But yeah, I'll be able to do it." I thought of the drunk blur I'd been in in Vegas. It might be a good idea to take a few shots beforehand, just to calm my nerves. My stomach curled in apprehension and arousal and maybe I wouldn't need any liquid courage at all. Maybe I'd be ravenous for it. I thought of the way I felt when I saw the photo he'd taken on his phone. How raw and hot it had been. The burst of confidence it had given me. How alive I had felt.

I rolled onto my side and propped up my head with one hand. "So, if a guy is watching us... where are you thinking he'd be? Outside?" I glanced at the bedroom windows, which were half-covered by bougainvillea bushes. If someone tried to watch us through them, he'd be eaten up by poison ivy, cobwebs and thorns. Which brought them into our bedroom. My gaze settled on the loveseat that was framed by the two windows and half-covered with folded clothes and shoes. I tried to picture a man sitting there, his eyes on me.

It seemed awkward. Like, really awkward. Would he jerk off? Just sit there and stare?

"They could be in the bathroom," Easton suggested. "Looking through the cracked door."

I wasn't in love with that idea either. It seemed creepy for a man to lurk in the dark, his face pressed against the crack. And then I'd have to clean the bathroom. I couldn't feel sexy with my blackhead cream screaming at them from the counter. "What about Aaron?" I lowered my voice, though if he could hear any of this, we were already fucked five different ways. "Is this guy just going to walk by him and into our bedroom? How are we going to explain that? And where are we even finding this hypothetical guy?" I sank onto my back, feeling overwhelmed by the implementation details. This was the issue with being a Capricorn. We thought through things too much.

"You realize the easiest solution to all of this, right?"

"No." Yes, but I wasn't going to voice it.

"We just do it with Aaron."

A traitorous bolt of arousal sang through my body, one deeper and stronger than anything I'd experienced in the last hour with Easton. Just his name, just that forbidden possibility, and my body hummed to life. I studied the couch and pictured him sitting on the edge, his body hunched forward, his gaze hungry. Energy would fly from that side of the room. My skin would heat with just the knowledge that he was there. Everything would be more intense, each thrust deeper, each orgasm more piercing. I let out a shaky breath. "We can't do it with Aaron."

"We can. He hasn't been with a woman since the last time Becca broke him off a piece, which was four months ago. I wouldn't be surprised if he's stealing your Victoria Secret catalogs just to have something to jerk off to."

"It'd be so awkward with him."

"It really wouldn't. Elle, you're comfortable with him. You know Aaron. If you farted in the middle of us all fucking around, you'd look at him and laugh."

"I never fart," I interjected with a smile, because he was right. We would all laugh about it, and I wasn't sure if that was more of a reason to approach him or less.

"Hey." His hand found mine under the sheet. "With him, if it's awkward, you can just come out and say it and he'll leave. Probably make some bullshit crack about our sex life on his way out." He grinned and I considered the idea again, letting the possibility actually breathe.

I inhaled, a shiver of excitement tingling through me. "Walk me through everything, starting from how you'd bring it up to him."

And then my scatterbrained husband, who could barely program our garage remote, laid out the guideposts for a situation that might actually work. I laid on my side and watched him speak, his voice lulling me into a gradual but deep sleep, my dreams filled with erotic half-whispers of time.

25

I sank into the hot water and closed my eyes, forcing my limbs to relax, trying to find a heartbeat that wasn't pounding in my chest. My stomach flipped, tension pooling in my gut. Settling my head back on a rolled towel, I listened to the silence of the house and wondered where they were.

Wild Junction, listening to the band?

Twisted Mermaid, at the oceanfront bar, tipping back beers?

The Tavern, watching sports and eating wings?

What were they talking about? Did they have this same knot of apprehension or were they fine?

Wayland was at Chelsea's, her repeated offers to babysit finally accepted. It would be both his first and last visit at her house. That, I was certain. I'd already seen evidence of that when he'd tore into her backyard, across a bed of delicate perennials, then rolled with absolute glee through a mud puddle.

For the first night in a long time our house would be dog-free. No distractions. No scratches at the door, or whines from his crate. One variable, gone.

I turned my head and eyed the black satin strip of fabric,

hanging off the hook beside the makeup mirror, where one of our embroidered hand towels normally sat. I'd bought it at the local quilting store and took longer than I should have to pick it out. The first material, I'd finally decided, was too slick. I didn't want the silky texture losing grip and falling loose from its knot. The second material, too scratchy. One felt hot. One was too thin. Or, I'd mused, holding it up to the light, *should* it be thin? Did I want to be able to see a little through the blindfold? I'd imagined the fuzzy outlines of them approaching, gripping their cocks, and had needed to sit down for a moment. My arousal had tanked when the salesperson had waddled around the counter and peered at me through eyeglasses with sunflower frames and asked me if I needed any help.

Oh sure, I thought. *I'm looking for something to use as a blindfold while my husband and best friend take turns on me. Any suggestions for length and texture?*

Though that would have been a wild exaggeration of the upcoming events. This was baby steps. Aaron would watch—same as he did in Vegas—just not from outside the window. From in here. In our bedroom. Close enough for me to hear him. Close enough, if I pulled off my blindfold—to see everything.

I looked through the open door, the edge of our bed visible. The corner of the dresser. The loveseat, which I had cleaned off in preparation for tonight. There were fresh sheets on the bed, the floors were mopped, and all of the junk on top of our dresser had been swept into the top drawers. Lit tea light candles flickered from the bedside tables and window sills.

Maybe I should blow out the candles. It was kind of a romantic vibe, and that certainly wasn't the mood I was going for.

Though what mood *did* someone go for in this scenario?

And if I blew out the candles, then the room would be too dark. Lighting a bedside table would be way too much light, and while I was comfortable with my naked body, I didn't want it to be seen under strong lighting by anyone other than E.

I studied the ceiling tiles. The house was too quiet. Even the air conditioner had shut up. This wouldn't work. What if it was like this during the event? Should I put on music? My sleep machine? Would the sound of crickets and ocean waves be distracting?

I rolled right and reached for my phone, careful not to drop it into the water. Opening up my texts, I sent one to Easton.

Let's cancel this. The house is too quiet. I can't figure out the bedroom lighting. I can't tell if I'm hungry or nauseous.

I saw the moment he read the text, then endured the long wait while he composed a response.

If you want to cancel, we will. No pressure. But both of us are horny as hell and no one will be listening or looking at anything but you.

Urgh. I set the phone on the floor next to the tub and sank into the water, fully submerging myself.

26

"How did we get into this shit?" Easton sat at the seat by the water, a corona bottle in hand. "You divorced, my wife waiting for us at home? We were supposed to be bachelor kings. Well," he corrected with a smile. "I was gonna be a king. You had a very likely chance of being in my entourage."

"Hey, we had one year of that. You almost fucked up my first job in that year. I think I missed more days than I showed up."

"Oh, right. *I* almost fucked up your job. Your arm was twisted so far back it was dislocated." Easton scowled. "Was it twisted when we went to Bimini?"

"No, but I think I felt a twinge in Cabo." Aaron rolled his shoulder and faked a wince. "Yep. Right there."

They laughed and then fell silent, watching a group of tourists pose for a photo at the surf. Easton's phone beeped and he glanced down at it.

"She's getting nervous."

"Think she'll back out?" Aaron tossed out the question as if he didn't care, but the evidence was in the tense way he straddled the stool, the constant bounce of his knee, and the fact that he was on his third beer, the label half peeled off.

"Nah. She'll come through. She's just second-guessing everything."

"Yeah. I get that. I'm nervous as fuck."

Easton studied him. "You know we can just call this off. I can go back alone and take care of her solo."

"No, I want it. It's just—" he came off the stool and stood, pulling down on one pocket of his jeans and readjusting himself. "It's just stressful. How in the hell are you so calm?"

Easton grinned. "She's my wife, dude. There's not another person on the planet I'm more comfortable with. And I trust you with her. If it was a stranger, someone I was worried was going to be rough with her, or an asshole—yeah, I'd be concerned. But you'll be cool, assuming you can keep your dick hard."

"Funny." Aaron winced as he carefully maneuvered back on the stool. "That isn't going to be a problem. I've been a steel rod for the last two days. I'm more concerned with coming the minute she touches me."

"If she touches you." Easton corrected. "She might just want you to watch."

"I could listen through the walls and it'd still be the most inter-action my dick's gotten in four months."

"Yeah, we need to get you out there. You had game at one point."

Aaron winced. "I'm just going to lay low for a bit until the dust settles on this divorce. You don't what a Jewish mother is like. I swear, she's yelling at me right now, from West Flag. She doesn't stop, EVER. And my next girl has to be Jewish. Otherwise my life is going to be a living hell. I told you what she did with my stuff right? How she had movers pull everything from my—Becca's—house and put it in her garage? She hasn't given up hope that I'll move back into my old room."

"Okay, so we find you an apartment and a Jewish girl. A kinky one." Easton winked at him. "The girl, not the apartment."

"Let me survive tonight first. With everything you did in college, you're used to this shit. I'll probably fill up my sexual quota after thirty minutes inside your bedroom and be set for a year." He tilted back his head, stretching his neck. "The apartment, on the other hand—I wanted to see what you thought of me moving in with Chelsea."

Easton coughed in the middle of his sip, and set down the bottle to pound at his chest. "Chelsea?" He swallowed, his eyes tearing, then let out another throat-clearing bark. Grabbing a tiny square napkin, he swiped at his mouth. "In her house?"

"She's got the room. And it'd just be for a few months, until I find something to buy."

"I don't know..." Easton mused. "It's just... Chelsea."

"I know. It's why I'm still sleeping with a small horse every night."

"Hey, you're the one who let Wayland in the bed. We make him sleep on the floor."

"I'm just thinking—after tonight—it might be weird, me still living there." Aaron glanced at him.

"It might be." Easton shrugged. "But I told you what she said. This is a one-time thing. Just to see if she likes it."

"Or if you do," he pointed out. "You might deck me the minute I touch her."

"Good point. With your glass jaw, we could fuck over your body and just wake you up at the end."

Aaron rubbed his palm over his jaw with a wince. "Maybe I don't have the balls to do this."

The phone beeped again. Easton glanced at the display, read the text, then stood. "Well, find them and let's go. It's time to get home."

27

I was in our bedroom, flat on my back on the bed, when I heard the front door open. Sitting up, I reached for the glass of champagne and took a quick, nervous sip.

Floorboards creaked and shoes sounded against the wood as they came closer. I slid to the edge of the bed and held my breath, staring at the dark corner where the door was.

This was crazy. Stupid. Really really awkward. I took another sip and gripped the black sash tighter.

There was a knock at the two. Three quick raps. Our signal. I sat up straighter and watched the door swing open, and the strong silhouette of my husband pass through. He closed the door behind him.

"Hey."

I smiled despite my nerves. "Hey." He came to a stop before me and surveyed me. I fidgeted, smoothing down the lines of my dress.

"You look beautiful." He stepped closer, cradled my face in his hands and looked down at me. "Are you sure you want to do this?"

I nodded, my skin humming in anticipation. My fears mixing

with thoughts of what was about to actually happen. Aaron was standing just outside the door. Waiting to come in. "Yes. Are you sure he's okay with it?"

He laughed. "He's *very* okay with it. Trust me. Do you want to use the blindfold?"

"Yeah." I passed him the black satin piece and waited as he placed it over my eyes, tying it into a tight knot at the back of my head.

"Good?"

I nodded.

"Nervous?"

I nodded.

"Move to your knees. Spread them open."

It was odd, the loss of my bearings. I moved to the floor and found the king-sized pillow I'd put there, my knees widening as I sat back on my heels. My dress, a midnight blue cocktail number, pooled around my knees and I ran my hands over the deep cowl neck, making sure I was fully covered. The deep sound of his chuckle came from above me. "Suddenly shy?"

I stuck my tongue out and started when his hand closed on my chin, the rough pad of his thumb rubbing across my tongue. I bit gently down and his hand tightened on my jaw.

"Naughty thing," he chided. "I'll punish you for that." He pulled away his hand and I felt a chill at the exit, my body craving more of a connection. "Ready?"

I nodded, my hands fisting in the thin fabric of my dress, my nerves sharpened to an almost painful point. This was it. I was suddenly grateful for the blindfold, for the protection it seemed to give me. No uncomfortable eye contact. No interaction. I'd please and be pleased by Easton, and he would watch. Technically, I'd have plausible deniability that Aaron was ever in our room.

The click of his shoes sounded across the floor and there was the squeak of the heavy brass handle, the subtle change in the air as the door opened and a second set of footsteps sounded.

Creak.

Creak.

Creak.

I stayed frozen in place, tracking Aaron's journey as he moved to stand to my left, closer than I had expected. If I reached out, would I touch him? It was hard to judge the distance. Easton brushed against me and I reached out, feeling my way up his jeans. He undid his belt and our hands touched as he dragged the zipper down. "Take it out."

I obeyed, self-conscious as I worked his jeans and underwear down, then ran my hands softly up his muscular thighs and over his cock. It was already swollen and grew rigid quickly under my hands.

"Jesus," Aaron muttered from beside us. "I forgot how fucking big you are."

"She can take it all." His hand closed on the back of my head and gently pulled. "Show him, Elle. Show him how well you suck my cock."

Heat bloomed in my belly and my hands tightened, my mouth opening as the stiff crown of his dick pushed inside. I took the head, then withdrew, rolling my tongue around the tip before I went back down, further this time, my throat opening up for his width. Easton's fingers bit into my scalp, his pelvis tilted up, and I felt his thighs flexed. "Fuck, baby."

I worked my mouth faster, hollowing my cheeks as I pulsed on and off his cock, growing bolder as he grew stiffer. Had he ever been so hard? He'd certainly never been so bossy, his hand now fisted in my hair, his voice rough as he encouraged me on.

"Her dress." The request came from Aaron, his voice hoarse with need. "Can she take it off?"

Emboldened, I started to reach back, to undo the closure, but stopped when Easton's hand closed on mine, pulling it away. "Let us do it."

There was a whisper of communication, then Aaron moved into

the tight area between me and the bed, his pants brushing against my back as he sat, the mattress sighing from the weight.

"Keep sucking," Easton urged, the points of his fingers returning to my head.

I did, grateful for the distraction of the task, my skin heating in the anticipation and realization that Aaron was right behind me. His fingers brushed against the nape of my neck, smoothing my hair out of way and I almost groaned.

He stilled. "Is it okay if I undo this?"

I nodded, my mouth too full to speak. He undid the link and slid the fabric off my shoulders, the dress slinking to my lap, leaving my breasts bare. I gripped Easton in my fist and licked up the underside of his cock, flicking my tongue against the lip of his head. "Have him touch me. My tits."

Aaron didn't wait for Easton's response, his hands sliding down my sides and then around to the front. I felt his breath against my shoulder as he bent forward for further access, the bed squeaking as he moved off of it and onto the floor behind me. He must be kneeling behind me, the stiff fabric of his shirt brushing against my back as his big hands cupped my breasts. He was more gentle than Easton. More hesitant. His fingers ghosted over my nipples as if he was afraid to touch them. Under the faint contact, they hardened, desperate for more. I arched into his touch.

"You like that?" Easton rasped. "You like him touching you?"

I nodded and, against my tongue, his dick twitched in response. I pulled off his cock and gasped in a breath. "I love it."

"Fuck..." Aaron muttered from behind me, his touch growing bolder, and I moaned as he pulled on one nipple, then the next.

"That's enough." Easton's voice was hard and possessive, his cock pulled away from my mouth and replaced by his kiss. I rose on my knees, gripping his hair as he claimed me with a rough and savage kiss. As he broke away, I felt Aaron move to his feet and heard his steps sound against the wood as he came to stand beside Easton.

Both of them, before me. I hesitated, still up on my knees, my breasts goosebumping in the open air.

"Pull out your cock."

The sound of the zipper was so loud in the room. I was never so grateful for the silence, for the erotic click of the undoing, the rustle of his jeans, the jingle of his belt. Was this... was this actually about to happen?

"Jack off as you watch her."

I licked my lips, aware that Easton was giving me a chance to restrict Aaron to watching, or bring him deeper into the act. I hesitated, warring between what I desperately wanted and an ingrained resistance strengthened by a lifetime of society's expectations and opinions. Could I?

I cleared my throat. "I want to taste him."

Aaron inhaled sharply, and I felt Easton move closer. He leaned down and kissed my shoulder, then gently squeezed one breast. "Good girl. Now open up that perfect little mouth. I want him to feel how well you can take a cock."

My need unfurled, like a flag hitting the wind, eagerness surging through me as I reached out and found Aaron in the darkness. He stuck straight out, as stiff as Easton had been, and I explored him with my hands and then placed the tip of my tongue on his shaft.

"Jesus." He moved back, then came forward. His hand touched my head, then he abruptly pulled his dick away.

"Should I stop?" I tilted my head up as if I could see him.

"Fuck no. I just..." He let out a breath. "God, you're hot. I just —" The toe of his shoe bumped against my knee. "Just go slowly. Please."

I inched forward on my knees and took my time, letting my tongue play along his seams and girth. He was thinner than Easton, but almost as long. His dick was like his build, strong and tall. I circled the head of him with my tongue and then worked him into my mouth, slowing the process down further as he sharply inhaled.

"I don't know how you do it, E. I'm about to fucking come just from watching her take my cock."

"I know. Her mouth is insane." I heard the pride in my husband's voice as he pulled my left hand off Easton's thigh and put it on his own dick. I curled my fingers around his stiff shaft, swelling under their praise.

This was it. My fantasy come to fruition. I was between the two of them. Aaron's cock was in my mouth. My husband was harder than steel and I had never been so wet or aroused in my life.

"My turn." Easton's hand closed on the back of my head and I turned to him, taking him as deeply as I could, and then pulled off.

Returned to Aaron. Took him to his base, and incited a string of curses from his mouth.

Went back to Easton, my hand working over Aaron, my weight shifting from knee to knee as I repeated the process, back and forth between the two men. My pussy grew heavy with need, and I shifted, bringing my heels underneath me, the strap of one stiletto abused as I ground against the clasp, dragging myself across the metal bit and still frustratingly unable to make contact with my clit.

My husband noticed my need, and his hand tightened on my shoulder, stopping my movement. "Now, it's our turn."

28

I stood, still bare on top, my nipples still fiercely hard and itching for stimulation. Between my legs, I was wet, my body throbbing, every pleasure sensor on high alert. The blindfold was still snug, everything dark and every sensation louder as a result.

Someone's hand brushed down the middle of my back. A slow finger trailed around one nipple and then the other. Two hands settled on the back of my thighs and slid up, underneath the hem of the dress, taking their liberties across the curve of my ass. Was it Easton or Aaron? Before this moment, I would have sworn that I'd recognize Easton's touch anywhere. But now, in the dark, everything was beginning to twist and mix into an unknown cocktail of eroticism.

It should have terrified me. A different woman would have held back. I wanted more.

A tongue flicked across my nipple and I reach out instinctively, capturing the head and pulling it onto my breast. Not Easton's short tuffs. This was coarser hair, and a thrill shot through me at the knowledge that it was Aaron who was now taking my nipple into his mouth. Aaron whose hands were cupping my breasts.

Aaron who was stepping closer, his clothes brushing against my skin, his groan vibrating out from his tongue. I pulled at his hair, bringing his mouth to my other breast, and pinched my eyes shut at the desperate need that flooded through me.

"Easton," I choked out. "I need more."

"Get on the bed."

Aaron withdrew and Easton pulled at my waist, bringing me back. I stumbled, then felt the bed behind me and sat.

There was movement. Items rustled. Something splashed. A shoe fell. A light brush of air moved across my skin as the fan came on. Bare feet slapped the floor. I started, then relaxed as Easton's mouth brushed mine, then kissed me deeper, a splash of champagne on his tongue.

He moved to my ear, kissing the lobe, then whispered into it. "Ready?"

"Wait." I hesitated, turning an idea over in my head before I put it into action. Was I ready? Was I sure?

But I was. I wanted more, and part of that included sight. I reached up and picked at the knot of satin at the back of my head, working it loose, the fabric falling around my neck. I pulled it off, dropping it to the floor and opened my eyes.

Easton stood directly before me, gazing down as if he wanted to both worship and devour me. I didn't look for Aaron, didn't do anything but reach for the glass in Easton's hand, tilting back the delicate flute and filling my mouth with the bubbly contents. An incredulous smile crossed his face, and he really was too beautiful at times. My eyes dragged down the stiff white fabric of his shirt and found his cock, jutting through the open bottom, bobbing suggestively before me. It twitched and I grinned. He was beautiful...and so naughty.

I didn't pull from Easton's eyes but could feel Aaron in the room, silently watching us. Waiting.

"Are you sure about this?" Easton put his finger under my chin and lifted it until my eyes met his. I wet my lips, the taste of champagne still on them, and nodded.

"Open your knees."

Gripping the edge of the bed, I parted my legs, the silky fabric of my dress clinging to my inner thighs.

He sank to his knees before me. Running his hand down to my calf, he gave the muscle a possessive squeeze before undoing the satin strap of my right stiletto. Carefully, he removed the shoe and set it aside, then moved to the left. In the dim bedroom light, I watched his features tighten in attentive concentration as his strong hands made quick work of the delicate heels. From somewhere to the left, Aaron let out a soft cough and every inch of my body tightened.

My bare feet settled on the wood floor as he ran his palms reverently up my bare legs, stopping at my open knees. His gaze flicked to mine. "Wider," he said hoarsely, and pushed them further apart.

I yielded, allowing him to stretch my legs open and lift my dress, draping it outside my knees so that I was fully exposed. He smiled when he saw my lack of panties, and ran a tender hand across my damp folds. His fingers spread me, then pushed so deeply inside that the platinum glint of his wedding ring disappeared. I gasped at the intrusion—finally—and his eyes darkened at how wet and needy I was. "Tell me what you want."

I met his eyes. "Him."

He swore and his fingers withdrew, then pushed back in, pumping across my neediest point. "Where?"

"Right here. On our bed." My eyes dropped and I could see the instant and stiffening response of his cock.

"When?"

I looked past him and at Aaron, my stomach tightening as I saw him hunched against our dresser, his face turned to me, his hands gripping the edge of the mahogany. Our eyes met and he stood, reaching back and pulling his shirt over his head, his face tight with hunger and want.

Hunger. Want. And expectation. It was a fierce and heart-stopping combination, the look one I'd never seen on him, the heat in his eyes all but searing through my skin. Naked, he stepped forward and my knees opened wider, welcoming him in.

I dug my nails into the fabric of Easton's shirt. "Now."

29

Aaron came forward until he was beside E. His hand closed on my left foot, Easton's closed on my right, and they brought my legs up, my back hitting the bed, my body open. Between my legs, Easton's other hand continued its movement, working faster as he pumped his fingers in and out of me. I met his eyes and they burned into me, his face tight with arousal, watching me as my body tightened, my orgasm close.

I clutched at his shoulder, my legs trembling. Aaron moved closer, his eyes on Easton's hand, and I felt almost dizzy at what he must be seeing. He reached out and cupped my breast, his fingers rolling over the nipple. I closed my hand over his, trapping it on the breast. "Squeeze it," I panted. "Harder."

"She likes it rough," Easton bit out. "Pinch them."

"I'm gonna—" I pinched my eyes tightly shut, feeling the orgasm approaching. Pushing out with my legs, I arched into E's hand, my breasts lighting on fire as Aaron pinched my nipple tightly. His bare dick poked into my leg and I broke, stiffening as the orgasm crashed, then swelled, then broke. I let it happen, knowing that Easton would soften his touch, that he'd slide another finger in when I needed it, that he'd hold me in place if I slipped off the bed and onto the floor.

When I opened my eyes, Aaron was pulling away from me and ripping open a condom wrapper. I watched through hooded eyes as he brought the latex ring to his cock and saw the tremble of his hand as he tried to work it over the swollen head. "Hey," I reached out and gripped his arm. "No rush."

Glancing up, he gave me a sheepish smile. "Honestly, it's the first time I've put a condom on in four years. I'm rusty. And nervous."

I laid back and waited, caressing my bare breasts, my confidence emboldened by his nerves. Turning my head, I saw Easton standing at the side, his gaze on me, eyes burning with heat.

"Put your fingers in yourself," he ordered. "Show him how wet you are."

I flicked my gaze to Aaron and slowly ran one hand down my stomach and across the thin strip of hair between my legs. I pushed a finger in, then a second, opening my legs and showing him the tight fit around my knuckles. His eyes followed the motion, and his breath shortened as he stroked his cock in rhythm with my fingers. "Fuck me," I begged. "Please."

Easton hissed, moving forward, and I turned my head, watching as he stalked up to the side of the bed, his hands flexing at his side.

"E..." Aaron gritted, his hand gripping my thigh, the head of his cock bumping against my soaked opening. I moaned, opening my legs wider, urging him inside me, as my eyes locked with Easton's. He looked lethal. Deadly. I thought of his words, that he'd kill anyone who touched me. I reached out and wrapped my hands around his cock, and found it as hard as glass.

"Do it," my husband grunted. "Put it in her. I want to see her face when you do." He leaned forward, his hands braced on the bed beside my head, and stared at me, his hips thrusting as he worked his cock in and out of my fist. "You're so fucking hot," he whispered. "You have no fucking idea how you have ruined me."

"I—"

Aaron thrust inside of me. I gasped, Easton swore, and everything spun into one delicious and erotic blend. With one simple thrust, there was a break, a moment where Easton's fury faded, where my confidence soared, where every awkward nerve fled in the presence of mutual pleasure.

My hand tightened on Easton's cock, his mouth closed on mine, and Aaron grabbed my legs.

It was the same, yet different. He wasn't as smooth as Easton. Not as confident. Jerky at times. Pausing at others. He was greedy with his eye contact, staring at my body as if he had never seen a woman naked before. I loved it. I devoured it. I performed for Easton and was instantly addicted to the possessive glower on his face, the pace of his motion. He furiously fisted his cock, jerking his hand over the erection as he stood beside us, his gaze stuck to our movements, his eyes dark with need.

When I came, Easton almost came off the floor. He dropped his cock and hissed through his teeth, crossing his arms over his chest as he urged Aaron on. I thrashed, I clawed at Aaron's arms, and when I saw the pre-come drip from Easton's cock, my pleasure hit a new peak of ecstasy. I was coming down, the room spinning, when Aaron stiffened.

"Shit, I'm going to come." Aaron bit out the words and yanked his dick out of me, stripping off the condom. Easton didn't hesitate, taking his place in between my legs. "Where should I—"

"On my face," I reached toward him from my place on my back. "Here. Please."

"Are you sure?" He moved forward as he spoke, his handsome face pinched in concentration, his hand gripping his cock.

"Yes. Please." My head dropped back as Easton pushed inside of me. Bigger. Barer. The difference between the two was noticeable and I met his eyes and bit back a smile at the cocky look on his face. He knew. My husband always knew, and it'd be annoying if that beautiful cock wasn't fully mine.

"Did you like when he fucked you?" Easton asked, his dick dragging in and out of me, slower than I liked it. I pumped my hips, trying to fuck him back, and he shook his head at me. I scowled at him and he grinned. "Did you like when he fucked you?" he repeated slowly.

"Yes," I gasped. "I loved it."

"Tell him." He nodded to Aaron, who stood by my head, his hand jerking over his cock.

I lifted my gaze to Aaron. "I loved it when you fucked me." Between my legs, Easton increased his speed, rewarding me. "Your cock felt so good inside of me."

"Jesus," Aaron swore, his eyes pinned to my face, his strokes growing shorter and faster, working over his glistening head.

"I loved having your cock in my mouth." I grabbed my breasts, pushing them together, my skin warming at the searing force of his stare, his full attention on every move, every word. "I loved having your mouth on my tits. I loved—"

"Fuck, I'm going to come." Aaron panted out the words, moving closer, his dick pointed at me as if it was a sword. I opened my mouth, sticking out my tongue, my body and breasts bouncing from Easton's thrusts.

"Please," I begged. "I want it so badly."

He groaned, his face pinching, and I jumped when the first shot landed on my cheek. The second, my mouth. The third hit somewhere over my head. I grabbed him and sat up, burying him down my throat, my eyes tearing at the depth. His hand palmed my head, a guttural sound ripping from him as he thrust into my mouth.

I gagged and Easton gripped my hips tightly. "Fuck, Elle. Do that again."

I came off his cock, took a deep breath and then went down again, the taste of his come slightly bitter, my throat slick with spit and juice, and gagged again, harder this time.

"I'm coming." Easton rammed into me with short rapid strokes, jack-hammer fast. Aaron's hands closing on my breasts, squeezing them, and my own orgasm chased Easton's down.

"Don't stop!" I cried wildly, feeling his release and desperate for my own. "Don't stop!"

He didn't, and my hand and mouth fell away from his shaft as I flopped back against the bed, my body binding and tightening into one exquisite ball of pleasure.

"Elle...." Easton warned, but it didn't matter. It didn't matter because I was rolling, my body flexing underneath his cock, the spasms of pleasure so pure, so intense, that it felt like a drug. A painful, beautiful, piercingly exquisite drug.

When it finally stopped, I went limp and Aaron's hands softened, then released. Easton stayed inside of me, but rolled forward, bringing me onto his body, and laying me across his chest. His leg wrapped protectively around me, and I heard the soft sound of the door opening, then closing as Aaron left.

"Wow," Easton said quietly, his heart thudding beneath me.

"Yeah." I closed my eyes and sagged against his chest, my body cooling as our heartbeats gradually slowed to normal.

Wow.

30

Thirty minutes later, my heartbeat had recovered, Aaron's side of the house was quiet, and my fears of an awkward post-threesome fight had dissolved. I'd expected repercussions. Guilt. Regret. Instead, I felt even closer to Easton. It reminded me of those weeks after Wakulla Springs, when I was so emotionally fragile, and he was so protective, and our dynamic shuddered into a new sort of form where we clung to each other and blocked out everything and everyone in order to heal over something we hadn't even known we had.

That intimacy had been born out of pain—this one out of pleasure. I watched as Easton flipped off the bathroom light. His hair was wet, a towel hanging around his neck. He was shirtless, plaid pajama pants low on his hips. He rubbed the towel over his head, then hung it on the hook by the bathroom door.

We'd showered together after the event, his rough hands suddenly soft, his touch tender as he'd run a soapy washcloth over my body. He'd kissed me under the spray, then turned off the water and dried me off before the sink, his eyes glued to the mirror, devouring the view. My skin had been pink from the hot water, alive from his touch, still tingling from what had just happened.

I scooted over to make room for him on the bed and reached for the glass of forgotten champagne. "The next time we have a three-some," I swallowed the last swig, then put the empty glass on the bedside table. "Let's make sure the guy doesn't live with us. Because I really want to stretch out on the couch with you right now, but feel like that might be a little awkward."

Easton chuckled, then sat on the bed beside me. "Yeah, the couch does sound really good right now."

"But awkward."

"Potentially awkward," he agreed. He pulled the blanket higher atop me. "How about I make us a fort, instead?"

"A fort?"

"Yeah. I'm actually really good at it. Not to brag or anything but in fourth grade, some people called me a king."

"A fort king?"

"It was a high honor at Presley Elementary."

"Fine." I rested my head back on the pillow. "Wow me with your fort skills. I give you..." I glanced at the bedside clock. "Five minutes to impress me."

"Damn, a time limit." He rolled off the bed and stood. "Way to make it challenging."

"Take longer than that and I'll be asleep." I yawned.

Six and a half minutes later, I was in a curtained box of mismatched sheets, the fabric draped over the headrest, tucked in a dresser drawer and bungee-cord tied to a dining room chair. A flashlight was cupped between us, extra blankets and pillows added to the bed, and the effect was innocent and sweet. Which was funny, considering everything that had happened in this room tonight.

"What do you think?" He pressed a kiss to the top of my head and pulled me tighter against his chest. I sank into his hold, my eyes closing as I inhaled the scent of him. He smelled like me, like sex and cum and champagne. But also, like home. Comfort. Strength.

"I think it's the best fort I've ever seen in my life. You definitely win fort king, despite going over the time."

"Will you be my fort queen?"

I smiled against his chest. "Is that a proposal?"

"It is. And look." He brought something out from underneath the blanket. "I even have a ring."

I laughed at the paperclip, bent into a circle, with a crooked mass of metal at the top. "Wow. Where did this come from?"

"To be honest, it's the only reason I missed my deadline," he said soberly. "It took almost two minutes to make. But I couldn't risk another proposal without a ring."

"I love it." I worked the ring onto my bare right ring finger and admired its glow under the flashlight's weak beam. "And I love you." I turned my head and took a gentle kiss.

"I love you too, my fort queen." He smiled and brushed the hair away from my face. "So," he said hoarsely. "What now?"

"You mean with this? Like what we did tonight?"

"Yeah." He pulled me higher on his body, then wrapped one leg around me.

"I don't know," I admitted. "Did you enjoy it?"

"Yeah. I don't have to ask if you did." He grinned down at me. "So what does that mean for us?"

"That's a good question," I played with the ring. "I guess we'll figure that out as we go."

"I think we filled Aaron's sexual quota for the year."

"Ha." I leaned my head against his shoulder. "He handled it well. How super awkward is this going to be tomorrow morning?"

"I'll be there. It won't be awkward. I'll make a joke and break the ice."

I groaned. "No jokes, please."

"I have one I've been saving just for this occasion. It'll be perfect. I promise you'll laugh."

"Tell me it now and I'll see if I laugh."

"It won't be funny now. It has to be authentically worked into conversation."

"I can pretty much guarantee it won't be funny then."

"Look, this is why I didn't want to do a threesome."

"What do you mean?"

"If I wanted to disappoint two people, I'd have just had dinner with my parents."

"Please tell me that wasn't the joke."

"I can see the edges of your mouth turning up. You gotta admit, it's funny."

I pinned my lips together to hide the smile that really wanted to come out. "It's super lame. We wouldn't have laughed at that."

"That's okay." He kissed the top of my forehead. "I got another one. It's almost as good. I'll whip that one out."

"Please don't whip anything out. I think I'm stocked up on bad jokes and penises for the week."

He lowered his head and gently nibbled on my neck. "You know, it was really odd, watching him with you."

I waited for more, my hands skating across his damp chest.

"It was so fucking hot, watching you. But also, so..." he paused, and I could see him searching for the right words. "It was like this possessive heat rippled through me. I wanted to shove him away from you but also hold you down while he fucked you. It was like a battle of emotions going on inside of me, and each side was pouring more gas on my arousal. I thought I was going to nut the minute you put your mouth on his cock."

Despite my sated state, his words sent a curl of pleasure through my body. I'd never felt so sexual before. So fearless. So desired. I stretched, then rearranged myself around his body, forming a tighter fit against his muscles.

Easton settled back against the pillows, his hand gently running through my hair as he flicked off the flashlight and set it on the bedside table. I closed my eyes and tried to understand what all of this meant for us.

I had loved it, more than I had expected to, and my mind clicked through every fantasy I'd recently enjoyed, assigning real scenarios to them, with Easton and I in each. I tried to shut off my mind and block out the images, tried to enjoy this moment with my husband. The sated stretch of my muscles, the contentment in my loins, the pleasure still tingling through my body.

Could we go back to a normal life? Could I be a normal wife? Could we have a normal marriage?

Or had everything just inexplicably changed?

The issue was, I wanted more. A lot more. And in that dark tent, in the sound of my husband's deepening sighs, I felt my sexual wings unfurl, their muscles tensing as if in preparation for flight.

It took me a long time to fall asleep and when I did, my dreams were full of pleasure and dominated by Easton's possessive and heated stare.

Do you want more of Easton and Elle?
I'm excited to announce that I'm writing another novel in their marriage! Twisted Marriage is coming in October 2019.
It is available for preorder now.

If you'd like to go ahead and read the first chapter, it is available at alessandratorre.com/tm
Please note: This chapter will end in a cliffhanger for some readers. Please avoid it if cliffhangers annoy you.

ACKNOWLEDGMENTS

Thank you to Jason Bell, who weathered my many questions about baseball, injuries, and high maintenance rookies. I hope you never read this book.

Thank you to Tricia and Yulanda, for reading each scene as it was written, and for your feedback, suggestions, and love for these characters. Tricia, you were beside me with every step of this novel, thank you for being the best PA and friend a woman could want.

Thank you to Marion Archer for her fearless edit and enthusiasm for this novel. Your timeliness, insight and professionalism never cease to amaze me.

Thank you to Sommer Stein, who created this beautiful cover while dealing with the most unhelpful and wishy-washy author on the planet.

Thank you to Amy and Tijuana for your beta reads - you are both the cream of the crop of beta readers and all of your catches, suggestions and questions helped me whip this baby into proper shape.

Thank you to Laurelin Paige and Kate Stewart, who convinced me to write another novel in this world.

Thank you to Torreville - my online reader group. Your enthusiasm for this book from the very beginning allowed me to really trust the concept and dive into the story, no holds barred.

And the biggest and best thank you goes to my husband. Without you, I would never have written a single word. I would never have known the true bond of romance, and I wouldn't be able to create stories that show it. Thank you for your continual inspiration, support, and love.

ABOUT THE AUTHOR

Alessandra Torre is an award-winning New York Times bestselling author of twenty-one novels. Torre has been featured in such publications as Elle and Elle UK, as well as guest blogged for the Huffington Post and RT Book Reviews. She is also the Bedroom Blogger for Cosmopolitan.com. In addition to writing, Alessandra is the creator of Alessandra Torre Ink, a website, community, and online school for aspiring authors.

If you enjoy Alessandra's writing, please follow her on social media, or subscribe to her popular monthly newsletter, where she hosts a monthly giveaway, along with writing updates, personal photos, and more.

www.alessandratorre.com
alessandra@alessandratorre.com

facebook.com/alessandratorre0
twitter.com/readalessandra
instagram.com/alessandratorre4

ALSO BY ALESSANDRA TORRE

Looking for another sexy read?

Hollywood Dirt. (Now a Full-length Movie!) When Hollywood comes to a small town, sparks fly between its biggest star and a small-town outcast.

Blindfolded Innocence. (First in a series) A college student catches the eye of Brad DeLuca, a divorce attorney with a sexy reputation that screams trouble.

Black Lies, the New York Times Bestseller. A love triangle with a twist that readers couldn't stop talking about. You'll hate this heroine until the moment you love her.

Moonshot, the New York Times Bestseller. Baseball's hottest player has his eye on only one thing—his team's 18-year-old ballgirl.

Tight. A small-town girl falls for a sexy stranger on vacation. Lives intersect and secrets are unveiled in this dark romance.

Trophy Wife. When a stripper marries a rich stranger, life as a trophy wife is not anything like she expects.

Love, Chloe. A fallen socialite works for an heiress, dodges an ex, and juggles single life in the city that never sleeps.

Made in the USA
Lexington, KY
27 September 2019